MAYBE THIS IS EVERYTHING

BY

JOSÉ F. NODAR

Northport Booksellers / Spring Farm NSW Australia

Spring Farm NSW Australia / José F. Nodar First Edition

ISBN 978-1-7640642-8-6 – Paperback
ISBN 978-1-7640642-9-3 – E-pub
ISBN 978-1-7640654-7-0 – Audiobook

This novel is dedicated

In loving memory of my wife,

Miriam Vassallo Nodar,

and her enduring presence.

You are always in my thoughts.

For anyone who's ever loved deeply, lost fully, and still found
the courage to begin again.

TABLE OF CONTENTS

MAYBE JUST COFFEE

The thing about ordering coffee is that it always feels like a performance. Especially here at Bean There, the oddly hip café tucked inside Brindle's Book Nook.

The line snakes around a display table of new paperbacks, and as always, I rehearse my order three people ahead of my turn like I'm preparing for a Broadway audition. Medium flat white, extra hot, one sugar. Is that too much to ask? I think to myself.

And yet, nine times out of ten, I get a lukewarm latte or something with almond milk.

Which I didn't ask for.

Which I never asked for.

But today, the coffee gods are mischievous.

I reach the counter and give my order with my usual half-smile, the kind that says I'm not high maintenance but please don't screw this up. The barista nods with that look that says, You and the twelve people behind you will all be forgotten by the time I blink.

I drift to the side, clutching my receipt, watching the books on the adjacent shelf. "New Fiction," it reads, although it should be called "New Titles to Remind You You're Not Writing Enough."

When my name is finally called, I step forward, grab the cup, and take a sip.

Wrong.

It's not even close.

It's iced.

I don't do iced coffee.

It tastes like coffee that died of exposure.

"Sorry," I murmur to the barista. "This isn't mine."

He barely glances at me. "It's what's on the sticker."

"But it's not what I ordered."

A shrug.

A flick of a towel over the espresso machine.

A passive-aggressive sip of his own drink.

I consider walking out. Let the universe win. But then she appears.

"Is there a problem?"

Her voice cuts clean through the caffeinated din.

She's not in a rush, but she's already in motion.

Short-cropped reddish-auburn hair.

Mid-forties, I say, with a beautiful smile and rolled sleeves.

Lanyard swinging around her neck like a librarian's talisman.

She's got the confidence of a magpie with a shiny thing—absolutely convinced it's hers and daring anyone to argue.

"Not really," I say. "Just a minor case of mistaken identity in beverage form."

She smiles.

Again, that smile.

It's not a performative customer-service smile. It's the kind that says she actually finds this mildly entertaining.

"I'm Harper Linton," she says. "Bookstore manager-slash-coffee wrangler when needed. You are?"

"Elliot Travers. Pretend author, frequent mumbler, and occasional over-reactor."

"Well, Elliot Travers, author mumbler," she says, taking the cup from my hand, "let's get you the right drink."

"I don't want to make a fuss," I say, immediately regretting it.

Why do I always say that?

It's my default setting. Avoid fuss at all costs.

"This isn't a fuss," Harper says.

"This is customer service. Or karma, depending on how your morning's going."

She places a new order herself.

To my surprise, she's fluent in barista.

The order is clear, calm, and somehow even polite, which feels like a minor miracle in the realm of café culture.

While we wait, she leans casually against the end of the counter.

"Writing anything I might've shelved?"

I laugh. "Not unless you've got a shelf for overly romantic novels and short stories and unpublished middle-aged memoirs."

"I do, actually," she says, straight-faced. "It's between True Crime and Books With Glaring Identity Crises."

That earns a proper smile from me, despite my best efforts to keep one eyebrow raised in quiet judgment.

By the way, I've perfected that look over the years.

"Let me guess," I say, "you used to be an actor, or a philosophy major. Or both."

"Neither. I just like stories. Even when they come with lukewarm coffee and cranky authors."

"I'm not cranky," I say too quickly.

"Well, maybe just lightly seared around the edges."

Another smile from her.

It should be illegal to look that confident before noon.

The barista slides a fresh cup toward us.

"Flat white. Extra hot. One sugar," he says, as if reading the side effects of medication.

Harper hands it to me ceremoniously. "To second chances."

"Or at least, hotter beverages," I reply.

I take a sip.

Perfect.

The kind of temperature that tells you someone listened.

"Well, Ms. Linton," I say, "thank you. You've restored my faith in humanity. Or at least in bookstore coffee."

"Happy to oblige," she says, stepping back. "Besides, we have to take care of the regulars."

I blink. "I'm a regular?"

"You hover by New Fiction every Tuesday and Thursday at 9:45. You browse, you sigh, you order a coffee, and you sit by the window pretending not to eavesdrop on people."

"That's disturbingly accurate."

She shrugs. "I pay attention. Occupational hazard."

"Also," she adds as she walks away, "you sometimes wear socks with typewriters on them. That's how I knew you were an author before you said anything."

I look down. Damn. She's right.

I watch her disappear between the shelves, greeting a customer and adjusting a book display like she owns the whole damn universe.

And maybe, in this little corner of it, she does.

I sit in my usual spot by the window.

Sip again.

The coffee is excellent.

The exchange was brief.

But something about it lingers longer than caffeine usually allows.

I open my laptop. For once, the page doesn't seem so blank.

Maybe it's just the coffee. Maybe it's Harper Linton. Either way, something's different today. And I'm not sure I mind.

THE ART OF EAVESDROPPING

It had been exactly one week since the "Coffee Incident," as I'd come to call it in my head — capital letters and all.

Seven days of obsessively replaying a five-minute conversation, analysing every syllable, every smirk, every flicker of eyebrow or glint of teasing in Harper Linton's voice.

And now, here I was again.

Same bookstore.

Same café.

Same internal monologue.

I didn't plan on seeing her.

That's what I told myself.

I just happened to be in the neighbourhood.

It's a lie so thin even I didn't believe it. I came because I wanted to hear her voice again.

She was shelving books near the front when I walked in, deep in conversation with a couple of customers who appeared to be debating whether their seven-year-old was ready for the Narnia series.

"Chronological order or publication order?" Harper asked, crouching beside a lower shelf.

The mother shrugged. "Does it matter?"

Harper stood and looked the woman dead in the eye with a dramatic seriousness that made me snort softly.

"It always matters. Publication order preserves the narrative arc. Chronological order is for the emotionally reckless."

The woman laughed. "Okay, then. Publication order it is."

I lingered near the Travel section, pretending to compare a guidebook on Bhutan with one on New Zealand, though the only travelling I'd done in the past six months was between my desk and the fridge.

Mostly the fridge.

I watched Harper as she handed over the books with the same self-assured grace.

She had a presence. Not just charm but command.

Like a general who knew the battlefield was made of stories and everyone else was still loading their muskets.

She looked up.

Our eyes met. I tried to look surprised, like I didn't know she'd be here.

Like I wasn't waiting for this moment like a teenager at a school dance.

"Mr. Travers," she said, striding over after the customers moved on.

"Back to hover by New Fiction, are we? Doing research, or just honing your lurking skills?"

I raised my cup.

"This is a reconnaissance mission. You know, for my next unwritten, uncontracted, and entirely imaginary novel."

She laughed, then tilted her head.

"Tell me, are you also a professional eavesdropper, or is that just a side hobby?"

"Technically, it's called 'passive listening.' It's essential for character development."

"Of course it is," she said, dropping into the armchair across from me without asking.

It didn't feel like an intrusion.

More like someone taking the seat they were always meant to occupy.

She reached into her back pocket and unfolded a slip of paper.

"I did some digging," she said, handing it over.

It was a handwritten list.

My books.

All of them.

Even the novella I'd self-published a decade ago and promptly tried to forget.

"You read all this?" I asked, feeling a curious mix of exposed and flattered.

"Some. Skimmed some. Tracked down the rest. You've got quite the voice, Elliot."

"I've been told I overuse em dashes and have a questionable relationship with metaphor."

"You do. And you do. But it works."

I didn't know what to say.

It's rare for someone to see your work, really see it, and still want to talk to you afterward.

"So, here's what I'm thinking," she continued, tapping the list.

"I'd like to do a small feature display in the store. We're overdue for a local author spotlight, and I think your books would do well. Especially if people knew you were the quiet guy always drinking coffee and watching them from the corner."

"I don't watch people," I protested.

"You narrate them in your head. Don't pretend you don't."

Fair enough.

"And if you're willing, I'd love to host a book signing. Nothing grand. Saturday afternoon. Free coffee. Possibly a bowl of cheese sticks if I'm feeling generous."

"You're serious?"

"Very. But I'll need a few weeks to rearrange the front tables and steal some shelf space from the trending TikTok nonsense. I'll be in touch."

I was about to ask what "in touch" meant when she beat me to it.

"Can I have your number?"

My brain did a full system reboot.

Somewhere in the background, a trio of teenage girls were arguing over romance tropes, but all I heard was that one sentence.

"Sure. Yes. Of course."

She handed me hers. It was warm.

Ridiculous that I noticed, but I did.

I typed my name and number, then hesitated before adding "(author, professional lurker)" to the contact field.

She looked at it and grinned.

"I'll let you know once I've sorted out the logistics."

She stood and tucked the paper list back into her pocket as if she were pocketing a treasure map.

"Thanks for stopping by," she added, then turned and vanished into the stacks like a magician mid-act.

I sat there with my coffee going cold, watching the empty chair she'd just left, and wondered how a conversation that short could leave such an aftershock.

The paper list, the book signing, the smile when I gave her my number. It all hovered around me like a shimmer in the air.

Harper Linton wasn't just confident.

She was deliberate.

Focused.

Like she saw things other people didn't.

And somehow, God help me, she'd seen me.

I stayed another hour, pretending to read a travel book I would not buy, my phone face-up on the table, just in case it buzzed.

It didn't.

But I wasn't disappointed.

Because I knew it would.

Eventually.

THE CALL AND THE QUESTION

The phone rings.

I don't rush to answer it. I wait. Let it ring once more, just long enough to keep some semblance of dignity. But inside, I already know. I looked at the screen.

It's her.

Harper Linton.

I can feel a grin pulling at the corners of my mouth like I've just been handed a long-lost manuscript and told I get to write the ending.

"It's early," I say as I pick up.

My voice tries to sound casual, but it comes out somewhere between caught off-guard and mildly delighted.

"Is it?" she replies. "It's almost noon."

"No, I mean early for the call. You said a few weeks."

"I also said I was impatient."

There's a pause.

Not an awkward one, more like the space between lines in a poem, something pregnant with meaning if you look too closely.

"I haven't finished the display yet," she says, "but I figured you could come by for something else."

My mind goes wild.

Something else?

"A poetry reading," she adds quickly, as if she heard me.

"A poetry reading," I repeat.

My brain's already sprinting ahead. Imagining shelves filled with my paperbacks, readers clutching them like holy texts, maybe even a local journalist or two taking photos while I pretend that I hate it.

But she's not calling about the signing.

Just the reading.

"It's tomorrow night," she continues. "Some local poets. Some good, some questionable, but all passionate. Figured it might help you get a feel for the space. You know. So, you're comfortable when it's your turn up front."

There's a pause again.

But this one's different. Tighter. More charged.

"And you'll get a sense of the crowd we draw. That's all."

That's all.

Of course.

Except it isn't.

"Right," I say, scratching at the back of my neck. "To get a feel for the book signing."

"Exactly," she says.

And yet I hear it. That tone. That small suggestion tucked neatly between the syllables.

Does she want to see me?

Or is she just doing her job with style, wit, and unnerving attentiveness?

"Poetry and I have a complicated relationship, like me and high-waisted jeans."

She laughs.

"Don't worry. No dress code. And no one's forcing you to read anything unless, of course, you get swept up in the moment and decide to share a haiku about your lunch."

I hesitate.

And that's when she says it.

"Elliot, come. Just so you get a feel of a book signing."

It's nothing, and it's everything.

She's making it easy.

She's making it about the store. But she's also giving me an out.

And an in.

I picture her leaning against the counter in her usual rolled-up sleeves and expressive eyebrows, pretending this isn't anything more than a professional invitation. But I've seen her version of professional. And this is something else.

"Okay. I'll be there."

"Good."

Then there's that pause again.

Like we both know the conversation should end, but neither of us quite wants it to.

I go first.

"Harper?"

"Hmm?"

"You said you have Tuesdays off, right?"

"I do."

"There's a place in Wexler, just the next town over. The Willow Tree. Quiet little restaurant, ridiculous soups, views of the hills that make you feel you're living inside a postcard."

"You're tempting me."

"I'm inviting you."

Another beat. A longer one this time.

Then: "Okay. Tuesday lunch it is."

I don't realise I've been holding my breath until she hangs up, and I finally let it go.

The poetry reading is not the sort of thing I usually attend.

It's standing-room-only, the scent of fresh coffee and worn paper thick in the air. Folding chairs are arranged in a semicircle at the front of the store, facing a small makeshift stage with a single mic and a red floor lamp that gives everything the glow of a confessional.

I spot Harper immediately.

She's working the room, of course, handing out programs, smiling warmly, fixing a crooked sign that says Verse & Voice: A Night of Local Poetry.

She sees me, nods once, and gestures to the back row where a seat waits.

The reading begins.

I listen to a nervous teenager rhyme "lonely" with "only" four times in one stanza. Then, an older woman who speaks as if she's unrolling memories from inside a cedar chest. There's a man with too much cologne and not enough metaphors, but the crowd is kind, the applause generous.

And Harper?

Well, she laughs, she listens, she claps. She's fully present for every single one of them.

I watch her more than I should.

And every time I think she's forgotten I'm here, her gaze drifts toward the back of the room and lingers.

After about two hours, everyone gets up and socialises a bit, grab a few the poetry books and head out the door.

I linger behind and speak with Harper.

It is just me, Harper and a few of her co-workers closing the shop for the night.

"Well, that was interesting," I say.

"It always is," she replies with that wonderful smile.

"Meet you on Tuesday as planned?"

She looks at me, gives me another of her smiles and says: "With bells on."

I walk out of the bookshop without a poetry book, but my imagination is doing its own stanzas.

THE SPACE BETWEEN WORDS

$$\infty$$

Tuesday arrives, and The Willow Tree is exactly as I remembered.

Low beams, stone fireplaces, an ambiance that whispers instead of shouts. The place where time softens around the edges.

I'm early. Of course I'm early.

I've already re-read the lunch specials three times and arranged the cutlery in a way that makes me feel marginally less unmoored. It's not nerves, exactly.

Just that itchy feeling behind the ribs when something might matter more than you're ready to admit.

When she walks in, the entire room recalibrates.

Not in a cinematic way. You know, no hair blowing in slow motion but in a subtle, internal way that makes me feel a little steadier just for seeing her. She's wearing a navy sweater and jeans; her auburn hair cascading over her shoulders.

Effortless, but precise. That's Harper in a sentence.

"You weren't kidding about this place, it's like dining inside a fairy tale."

"Wait until you try the tomato-basil soup," I say. "It's mythological."

She smiles, slipping into the seat across from me like she's done it a hundred times before.

We settle in.

Order drinks.

We laugh about the slam poet who accidentally knocked over the mic stand mid-stanza. She mimics the poet's expression, somewhere between panic and unshaken confidence, and I nearly choke on my mineral water.

But then something shifts.

It's in the quiet between bites.

The lull that isn't awkward, just heavier.

She's stirring her soup absentmindedly when she asks, "Do you still enjoy writing?"

And I answer, "I'm not sure."

It surprises even me, the honesty.

Usually, I offer the practiced shrug, the quip about deadlines or writer's block, something that glances off the truth without touching it.

But here, with her, my armour slips.

She tilts her head, studying me. "You've published seven books. That's not an accident."

"Maybe not, but lately, it feels like I've been writing on fumes. Like the words want to be somewhere else."

She nods slowly, eyes narrowing just a little. "Maybe the words are waiting for you to catch up."

I blink. "That's either incredibly insightful or just the right amount of vague to be comforting."

She smiles. "A bit of both."

We linger long after the plates are cleared.

The server floats by with dessert menus, but we wave her off.

The conversation is sweeter. And deeper.

Eventually, the talk veers into less curated territory.

"Were you ever married?" she asks, almost in passing, as if it's just another topic like her favourite films or preferred fonts.

I pause, then nod. "I was. For twelve years. Divorced six years ago."

She says nothing right away. She lets that small revelation settle like dust on an old book jacket.

"What happened?" she asks, and the way she asks it in a gentle, direct, not fishing but asking, which makes it feel okay to answer.

"Nothing dramatic. No scandal, no broken plates. Just two people drifting in parallel lines. We forgot how to meet in the middle. Or maybe we stopped trying."

She's quiet, and I can tell she understands something in that. Her fingers trace the rim of her water glass.

"My parents split when I was ten. Dad left for a woman who taught yoga and didn't believe in gluten. Mom stayed bitter and brilliant. She turned her anger into a career."

"Therapist?"

"Essayist," she replies with a dry laugh. "Turned our lives into material. She wrote a whole series called Solo Parenting and Other Acts of Vengeance."

"Ouch."

"She always said writing was her revenge."

"And yours?" I ask.

Harper looks at me for a moment, unreadable.

Then: "Mine's a kind of redemption, I guess. Not the writing, necessarily, more the bookstore, the conversations, the curation. Giving people's stories without turning them into weapons."

I nod, the weight of that sitting comfortably between us.

She's not just good with words. She's careful with them. And that, I've learned, is rare.

"It sounds as though you've been hurt in the past."

Harper takes a sip of her wine before answering me.

"My marriage to Robert was a mistake from the beginning, but being young, I did not see it. He was a cold, narcissistic person, and I did not see that. He did not value me; it took me ten years to figure that out before we divorced. I have two grown children, two girls. Ashley and Debra."

She glances down, suddenly shy. "Sorry. That got a little heavy for tomato soup."

"It's okay. Do not worry about it. We both understand what's not being said."

She chuckles. "True. But sometimes it's nice to say things aloud."

The bill comes.

I offer to cover it. She tries to protest, but not too hard.

"The next time it is on me. Fair warning—I tip in dessert."

We walk outside.

The air is crisp, and the leaves are beginning to turn, the trees giving up summer without apology.

"Thanks for lunch," she says.

"Thanks for coming."

We linger by her car.

Neither of us reached for the door.

The pause isn't awkward. It is intentional.

A space where something could grow.

"You know I've been thinking about the signing. I want to make it more than just a table and a stack of books. Something a little different."

"Define different."

"A conversation. You and a few readers. Maybe someone interviewing you. Something that feels personal."

I nod slowly. "You're good at that."

"At what?"

"Making things feel personal."

Her eyes don't flinch from mine. "I try."

And she means it.

Not in a flirtatious way.

In a truthful one.

Like she's been trying her whole life to connect with people in ways that last longer than small talk and end-of-receipt surveys.

We stand there for another breath.

Then she says, "I'll text you."

And just like that, she's gone.

Back home, I sit at my desk.

The sun filters through the blinds in long, golden strips, and my fingers hover over the keyboard.

I don't start a novel. Not yet.

But I type something. A single sentence.

"She asked if I still enjoyed writing, and I almost told her the truth."

Almost.

Then, after a minute, I add:

"But I think the words are starting to find their way back."

LISTS AND LATE NIGHTS

$$\infty$$

I t started with a meme.

A dumb one.

A cartoon avocado proposing to a slice of toast with a caption that read: Let's never split up.

I sent it to Harper on a whim.

It was past ten, and I'd just finished watching a documentary I can't even remember now. I saw the meme, thought of her laugh from lunch the other day, and hit send before I could question whether it was too late or too weird or just too much.

She replied three minutes later with: "I hate I laughed. But I did. Loudly."

Then she asked: "You're not asleep?"

"Are you?" I texted back.

"Touché."

And that was it.

The start.

The first late-night conversation that felt like it had always been there, waiting in the wings for us to stumble into it.

Over the next few nights, texting became a thing.

Not just memes or funny links, though there were plenty of those, but actual, meaty back-and-forth.

Observations about people.

Old stories.

Books we hated.

Songs we secretly loved.

She told me she once got kicked out of a yoga class for laughing during savasana (a resting yoga pose where you lie on your back with your arms and legs extended, palms facing up, and eyes closed).

I admitted to owning a pair of socks with Shakespeare's face on them.

On Thursday night, she called me.

No text warning.

Just the soft buzz of my phone lighting up on my nightstand with her name.

I stared at it for a second, like it was a fire I wasn't sure I should touch.

Then I answered.

"Hi," I said, voice lower and rougher than I meant it to be.

"Were you asleep?"

"No. Just thinking about Shakespeare socks."

She laughed.

"They sound dashing. Truly Elizabethan."

"Thank you. I try to bring a touch of 1592 to my ankles."

From there, we talked for an hour.

Maybe more.

I told her about the time I accidentally called my teacher 'Mom' in sixth grade. She told me her older brother once replaced all the photos on her phone with pictures of raw chickens, and she didn't notice for two days.

There was something so easy about it.

No spotlight.

No pressure.

Just us, in our own little after-hours pocket of the world.

My bravado came on Saturday night.

I was feeling bold or maybe a little unmoored.

I'd had a glass of wine. Or two. Okay, three. Maybe four. OK, it was the entire bottle, and I felt fantastic. I was sitting on my couch, phone in hand, scrolling through our text history. Something about it made me ache both hopeful and scared all at once.

So, I typed it.

"Things I Wouldn't Say on a Second Date But Want To:"

I didn't send it right away.

I stared at the blinking cursor, wondering if this would make her pull back. Wondering if I was about to ruin whatever strange, beautiful rhythm we had.

Then I hit send.

And added the list.

Dammit, I overthink everything. Like everything.

I secretly love romantic comedies and will quote When Harry Met Sally at inappropriate moments.

Sometimes, I worry I'm too boring to be truly known.

I haven't been in love in years.

I've dated. I've tried.

But that big, hit-you-in-the-chest kind of feeling?

Well, it has been a while.

I Google symptoms. It's a problem.

I think about legacy more than I should for someone who still forgets to do laundry until I'm down to mismatched socks.

I would absolutely get a dog if I knew I'd be good at it.

I get this weird ache in my chest when I see dads with their kids. Not jealousy. Just longing.

Sometimes, I pretend I'm on a cooking show when I make eggs.

I'm terrified of being truly seen and wanting it, anyway.

I pressed send again.

No take backs now.

Nothing for five minutes.

Then: "Wow."

Another minute.

"Give me ten."

I waited, phone face-up on the couch like a person.

My heart drummed in my ears. I started imagining all the ways she'd politely ghost me tomorrow. Or worse, be kind about it.

But then it came.

Her list.

"Things I Wouldn't Say on a Second Date But Want To: (Harper's List) PS – one at a time so read them slowly."

I sometimes walk around the house narrating my life in a David Attenborough voice.

I don't trust people who don't like carbs.

My parents' marriage was a mess, and I still flinch when people raise their voices.

I dated someone for almost three years and realised halfway through that I had been lonely the entire time.

I still have the ticket stub from the first concert I ever went to. I don't even like the band anymore. But I keep it.

I'm scared I'll become someone who settles.

I sleep with the TV on sometimes, not for the noise, but so I don't feel like I'm the only person awake in the world.

I once cried at an ad for paper towels. In a store.

I hate the idea that vulnerability is a weakness.

I think about what it would be like to fall in love again. Then I get scared. Then I think about it, anyway.

I read it once.

Then twice.

Then again, slower.

Each line a stone tossed gently into a still pond, rippling something open in me.

"That's the most beautiful use of ten text bubbles I've ever seen," I wrote back.

She replied with a heart emoji and then she added: "I can't believe I sent that."

"I can."

"Yeah?"

"Yeah. It was brave."

There was a pause.

A long one.

Then, her typing bubble popped up again.

"It feels like maybe we're doing something dangerous."

"Does it feel wrong?"

"No," she wrote. "Just like walking on a tightrope. But I don't want to get off it yet."

I let out a breath I hadn't realised I was holding. Then I typed:

"So, we hold hands while we walk the next time we meet for lunch or dinner. Deal?"

Her reply came almost instantly.

"Deal."

From there, something shifted.

Or maybe it deepened.

We said nothing too dramatic, nothing that would've felt like a declaration. But the undercurrent changed. It wasn't just flirtation or curiosity anymore. It was confiding. Leaning in. Letting the mask slip, slowly, carefully.

One night, she told me about her nephew and how he once called her "Auntie Arper" because he couldn't pronounce H's. She cried when he finally said her name correctly.

I told her about my mom, how she used to make pancakes in the shape of our initials, and how I couldn't bring myself to throw out her old recipe box even though I hadn't opened it in years.

She asked me what I was most afraid of.

"Waking up one day and realising I played it safe my whole life," I said.

She didn't reply right away.

Then:

"Same."

Sometimes, the silence between texts felt louder than the words.

Sometimes, the space was filled with just knowing she was there.

Awake. Thinking. Maybe about me.

Maybe about us.

It's funny how connection sneaks up on you. One minute you're sending memes about avocados, and the next you're sharing pieces of your soul you didn't even know you were ready to give away.

Every night, we reached a little further into the quiet.

We peeled back layers.

Not all the way.

Not yet.

But enough to feel like we were building something.

Something real.

I didn't know where it was going.

But for the first time in a long time, I wasn't rushing toward certainty.

I was okay floating in the middle, learning her rhythm, letting her learn mine.

And every time her name lit up my screen after dark, my world felt just a little less alone.

A little less safe.

And a lot more alive.

Then she said; "How about we meet at a friend's place. He has a gigantic rooftop that he has built up into a party place. My friend is having a small band play some oldies this Friday night and told me to come along and bring a friend. And he's ridiculous but lovable; just ignore half the things he says. You interested?"

I probably took over ten seconds to answer. You know, I was playing cool when I answered in the affirmative.

"Great. Meet you there. I will text you the address. 7:30 PM is OK for you?"

"Sure. Send me the address, and I will be there."

"See," I told myself, one layer at a time.

THE START OF SOMETHING

I never expect much from rooftop parties. They're always either too loud or too curated. Everyone pretending to be relaxed while wondering if their shoes are scuffed or if they use the wrong fork during the finger food round.

But when Harper invited me to one hosted by her friend and added (He's ridiculous but lovable, just ignore half the things he says), I said yes before even thinking.

Maybe because I wanted to see her in a different light.

Or maybe just see her.

I arrived with the usual wariness and a bottle of wine I hoped was overpriced enough to look thoughtful. The building was one of the converted warehouse type, all exposed brick and mood lighting. I took the elevator up to the rooftop and was immediately hit with the hum of conversation, the scent of something grilled, and laughter that didn't feel forced.

And then I saw her.

Harper, standing under a string of Edison bulbs, laughing at something a man next to her had just said. She was wearing a navy dress that floated around her knees and made her look like she'd wandered out of a dream and into someone's birthday bash.

The man beside her was tall. Broad-shouldered. Impossibly good-looking in a beachy, unbothered kind of way. My stomach twisted, just slightly.

She spotted me, smiled, and waved me over.

"Elliot!" she said, with a warmth that made everything else go momentarily quiet.

"This place is very rooftop." I looked around, buying time.

She laughed. "That's the correct architectural term."

"This is Theo," she said, nodding toward Mr. Tall and Charming. "Host, bartender, occasional DJ."

Theo grinned and gave me a fist bump. "Harper says you're funny. Let's find out."

And then he was gone.

Off to stir something in a pitcher while someone yelled his name from across the deck.

"Handsome guy," I said lightly, watching him go.

Harper raised an eyebrow.

"He's like a golden retriever. Lovely to be around, but not my type."

"Oh."

"Surprised?"

I shrugged. "Maybe."

"Good." She smiled mischievously. "Let's find the playlist before he plays John Mayer again."

We ended up wedged between a planter and a vintage speaker, analysing every song that drifted through the warm night air. Music turned out to be one of those sacred, Venn-diagram-crossing things for us with enough overlap to spark a delightful conversation, enough difference to argue.

I admitted to crying during a Julia Jacklin song.

She confessed she still had a playlist called "2007 Emo Breakdown."

I had no idea what the hell that was but just smiled because she was happy sharing that bit of information. I knew I had to Google that once I got back to my place.

The music started, and we slow-danced without realizing we were slow-dancing.

That's not a poetic exaggeration.

It actually happened like that.

One moment we were talking about how sometimes lyrics always sounded like a sad man trying to read you bedtime stories, and the next, some soft indie track had lyrics taken over the rooftop, and we were moving.

Harper takes her shoes off. I do not.

Hands lightly touching.

Bodies closer than usual.

The party faded, blurred.

Everything else receded into the background.

"You're good at this," she murmured.

"Slow dancing or talking nonsense about bands?"

"Both."

Her voice was warm.

Her eyes were warmer.

I was getting warm myself.

More drinks found their way into our hands.

The kind that tastes like nothing and sneaks up like everything.

We wandered toward a quieter corner of the rooftop, leaning against the railing and watching the city glitter below.

"I love this view," Harper said. "It makes all the chaos feel... held."

"Held," I repeated. "I like that."

We talked about family.

The weirdness of being at our age and still not sure if we were the grown-ups in the room. Her childhood bedroom had glow-in-the-dark stars on the ceiling. Mine had a framed poster of the solar system I used to stare at when I couldn't sleep.

Then I gestured too broadly while telling a story. Some ridiculous things about my high school band days and the glass of red I was holding tipped.

A neat, horrifying splash straight across my shirt.

"Oh no," I muttered, staring down at the spreading stain.

Harper blinked, then laughed. "You are an absolute disaster."

"It's part of my charm."

"Come on," she said. "I live just a few blocks away. We'll get you sorted."

I hesitated.

"Won't we miss more of Theo's obscure Swedish funk collection?"

"Tragic, but we'll survive."

We walked the few blocks in companionable silence.

The kind that felt full, not empty.

She lived in a small terrace house on View Street, with cracked tiles and potted plants guarding the door. The kind of place that immediately felt like someone lived there, not just occupied it.

Inside, she tossed her keys into a bowl shaped like a dinosaur and motioned for me to follow.

"Sit. Don't drip. I'll get something for you."

I stood awkwardly in her entryway, wine-stained and mildly mortified.

She returned, holding out a sweatshirt.

It was pink.

And it said I LIKE BIG BOOKS AND I CANNOT LIE across the chest.

I stared.

She grinned.

"It's either that or something with a unicorn. Choose wisely."

I peeled off my ruined shirt and pulled the sweatshirt over my head. It was warm and smelled like her laundry detergent — citrusy and soft.

"It suits you," she said, her eyes lingering for a beat longer than necessary.

"Are you mocking me?"

"A little."

We laughed.

But it lingered. That stillness again. That pull.

I should've said goodnight then.

Should've made a joke, grabbed my shirt, and left with dignity mostly intact.

Instead, I stepped closer.

"I'll bring this back," I said, tugging lightly at the hem of the sweatshirt.

"Clean?" she teased.

"Folded and everything."

And then she kissed me.

Not tentative.

Not polite.

But sure, and unhurried, and absolutely electric.

I kissed her back.

There was wine and night air and the ghost of a thousand almost-conversations in it. When we finally broke apart, she rested her forehead lightly against mine.

"Goodnight, Elliot," she whispered.

She stepped back, opened the door gently, and gave me one last look before it clicked shut behind me.

The walk back to my car was surreal.

The sweatshirt felt like armour and a memory all at once. I caught sight of myself in a shop window.

Rumpled hair, dazed grin, pink sweater and laughed.

What the hell just happened?

I replayed it all.

The dance.

The conversation.

The kiss. Especially the kiss.

I tried not to read too much into it.

Tried to keep my feet on the ground.

But the truth was, I was over the moon. Absolutely, unapologetically over the moon.

And that's when the danger starts with me—when I let the "what ifs" in.

What if this is the start of something?

What if we're not just late-night texts and rooftop banter?

What if she feels even a sliver of what I feel?

My heart raced ahead of me, spinning stories, dreaming futures, writing scenes in my head like a fool who's always one chapter ahead of reality.

Still.

As I opened my car door and sat behind the wheel, I couldn't stop smiling.

Because maybe the story was finally beginning.

And this time, I didn't want to skip to the end.

INTERSECTIONS

I'd like to say I played it cool.

That after Harper kissed me—really kissed me—I strolled back to my car whistling, calm and composed, already drafting a breezy "Had fun, let's do it again" text in my head.

But no. I practically skipped.

I walked into my home in a state somewhere between euphoric and completely deranged. I may or may not have fist-pumped the air when no one was looking. I definitely smelled the inside of that pink sweatshirt more than once. And when I stood in front of the bathroom mirror grinning like a guy in a toothpaste commercial, I knew I was hooked.

This was happening.

Something real. With Harper.

By noon the next day, I'd typed and deleted four versions of the same message. Something about dinner. About us. About moving from after-hours texts and rooftop flirtation into daylight. Into something more deliberate.

Finally, I settled on:

"I owe you dinner. Something with actual menus and silverware. Are you free this weekend?"

Her reply came fifteen minutes later: "Menus and silverware? You certainly know how to romance a girl. Saturday sounds perfect."

"I do. Meet you in front of the library, say 7:00PM?"

Her answer was one paragraph.

"Deal."

The library, which opened until 10 PM on Saturdays for author readings and other stuff that at this moment just did not sink into my mind, illuminated the street. I booked a cozy Italian place tucked away near it. The Italian restaurant had the kind with candles and red-checked napkins that screamed at you, and I knew they had a server named Paolo who took his pasta personally. It was a spot that didn't just serve food—it hosted moments.

Saturday came, and I wore the one shirt I owned that looked like I ironed it on purpose. I showed up five minutes early and waited outside, my palms weirdly clammy despite the cool breeze.

Then Harper arrived.

Effortless, as usual.

A green dress, brown boots, hair down. Like spring and rebellion and warmth all shared the same body.

Damn, she looked ravishing.

"You look like someone who holds doors and orders the excellent wine," she said.

"Don't be fooled. I'm a chaotic neutral in the wild."

She laughed, looping her arm through mine as we started walking into the restaurant.

It was all going perfectly. Too perfectly.

Which, of course, is when the universe reared its smug, ironic head.

We turned the corner—and there she was.

Laura.

My ex-wife.

She was walking in the opposite direction, hand-in-hand with a man I didn't recognise. Tall, broad-shouldered. Bearded. A Patagonia jacket kind of guy. The guy who probably climbs mountains as a hobby.

Our eyes locked.

I felt it immediately—like someone had dropped a lead paperweight into my stomach. Not because I still had feelings for Laura (I didn't) but because of the whiplash collision of past and present, the way your brain short-circuits trying to process two chapters of your life suddenly overlapping.

"Elliot?" she said, slowing.

"Laura, hi." I straightened up, subtly letting go of Harper's arm.

Laura glanced at Harper, then back to me. "Wow. It's been a while."

"Yeah. It has."

Her companion stood silently, polite but visibly confused.

I recognised that expression.

The expression that you think about if I need to punch this guy's face or shake his hand?

Laura turned slightly. "This is Ryan. Ryan, this is Elliot."

We shook hands awkwardly. His grip was firm. Mine was sweaty.

"And this is Harper," I said, gesturing beside me.

Harper, to her credit, stepped forward with a confident smile and extended her hand. "Lovely to meet you."

Her voice was smooth, unbothered. Like we'd just run into a neighbour, not the woman who once argued with me about salad spinners and who got to keep the Le Creuset Dutch oven.

"Likewise," Laura said, offering a smile that didn't quite reach her eyes.

There was a long moment of silence, all four of us suspended in that tight, too-small space of polite discomfort.

"Well," Laura said brightly, too brightly. "Enjoy your evening."

"You, too," I replied, just a second too late.

And then they were gone, strolling off into the evening like an ad for artisanal tea.

I didn't realise I'd stopped walking until Harper gently touched my arm.

"Hey," she said. "Breathe."

I exhaled long and slow. "Sorry. That was unexpected."

"You, okay?"

"Yeah. Yeah, I just—she's not someone I've seen in a long time. And definitely not someone I expected to bump into tonight. With you."

Harper nodded. "Ex-wife?"

I glanced at her, surprised.

"You pulled your arm away when you saw her," she explained. "And your face looked like you had just got hit by a mild but persistent wave of trauma."

"Fair assessment."

"Do you want to talk about it?"

"Not particularly. But I want to tell you, anyway."

We started walking again, slower now.

I shared with her the short version- my version of what happened anyway - how Laura and I had married young, how things had been good until they weren't, how we'd tried to fix what couldn't be fixed, how the divorce was not civil and left its scars deep in me. I kept my voice steady, even when my stomach hadn't quite caught up.

Harper didn't interrupt.

Didn't offer platitudes.

She just listened, really listened.

When I finished, she said, "Thank you for telling me."

"I didn't mean for tonight to be a meet-the-ghosts-of-relationships-past situation."

She smiled. "I'm glad I met her. Even in passing."

"Why?"

"Because now I know what your ex looks like, and I can confidently say I win."

I laughed—genuinely, surprisingly.

"Also," she added, "you were great. A little sweaty. But great."

By the time we reached the restaurant, the awkwardness had faded into something else.

Something lighter. I felt more settled, not less, having that strange moment out in the open.

Dinner was perfect.

We shared pasta, ordered wine with names we couldn't pronounce, and talked about everything and nothing.

I told her about the time I was living in the USA, and I accidentally crashed a quinceañera. She told me about her failed attempt to foster a cactus ("It died. A cactus. That's how low the bar was, and I still failed it.")

I watched her talk. Laugh. Sip her wine.

And I felt something I hadn't felt in years.

Ease.

Not the kind that comes from knowing someone for decades, but the kind that feels like maybe, just maybe, you've stumbled across someone who fits into the quiet corners of your life with no need to rearrange the furniture.

After dinner, we strolled back toward where we'd started; the city hushed around us.

"I'm sorry again about earlier," I said.

She shook her head.

"Don't be. People come with a history. Yours just walked by in a very stylish jacket."

"Was he stylish? I didn't notice."

"Elliot."

"Fine. A little stylish."

We reached her street and stopped in front of her door. The light from the lamppost cast a soft glow on her face.

"This was a fantastic night," I said.

She nodded. "Even with the ex-wife cameo."

"Especially with the pink sweatshirt still in my car," I added.

She grinned. "You keep it?"

"I was going to return it clean. Folded. With ceremony."

"Maybe keep it a little longer," she said softly.

"Why?"

"So, you have an excuse to come back."

I looked at her. Really looked at her.

And then I kissed her.

Not a chaotic, party-ending kiss.

Not a bold, wine-fuelled one either.

Just a quiet, long, deliberate kiss with a feeling you get when you want to turn a page you've waited a long time to read.

When we pulled apart, she whispered, "Goodnight, Elliot."

"Goodnight, Harper."

She stepped inside.

The door clicked shut.

And I stood there, grinning like a fool under the lamplight, my chest full of possibilities and trouble and all the dangerous what-ifs that make life worth living.

A START

∞

It started with the rain.

Not the kind you plan for.

The kind that surprises you sideways and sudden, slipping between jacket buttons and good intentions.

We were halfway through our second date, which had begun as a casual afternoon coffee and stroll through the park. I brought an umbrella, but not the kind that actually works. It flipped inside out in the first gust like it was auditioning for a slapstick reel.

Harper laughed, which helped.

At first.

"It's just rain," she said, her eyes bright under the hood of her jacket. "We won't melt."

We walked anyway.

Shoulders bumping, fingers brushing. I thought it felt romantic, cinematic even. Two people defying weather and awkward first dates and ex-wife run ins.

But the quiet settled in wrong.

Not the comfortable kind.

The sharp kind.

The kind that feels like you're both holding a word on your tongue, daring the other to say it first.

We stopped under the overhang of a closed flower shop.

Rain spilled from the awning in sheets.

Harper looked at me, really looked at me, with that intense stillness she has when she's thinking something through.

"Can I ask you something?" she said.

"Of course."

"Why do you do that thing?"

I blinked. "What thing?"

"That disappearing act. Emotionally."

I stared at her, confused. "I, what? I don't..."

"Yes, you do," she said, not unkindly. "You go all in — funny, warm, present, and then the moment something real hovers near the surface, you retreat. You go quiet. You look somewhere else."

"That's not fair," I said, my voice sharper than I meant it to be. "Maybe I'm just trying to be careful."

"Exactly," she said. "Careful is safe. Safe is distant."

I folded my arms.

Not to be defensive.

Just to keep from shaking.

"Right. And you're the poster child for emotional availability?" I spoke.

"You treat vulnerability like it's a game of hot potato. God forbid, you hold on to it too long."

Her face stiffened.

The hurt flashed quickly before she turned her head slightly, like she needed the rain to cool her off.

"That's rich," she said.

"Coming from someone who only seems to show up fully when it's convenient or flattering."

"That's not true."

"No?" she said, stepping away from the overhang.

"Then tell me something genuine right now. Something messy."

I opened my mouth.

Closed it.

The words were there, so many of them.

But they clogged in my throat, tangled in pride and fear and the dull, familiar ache of messing something up just when it starts to matter.

"I..." I started.

She waited. Eyes steady. Rain collecting on her lashes.

"I'm scared I'm not worth trying for," I said finally.

"Okay? There. I said it. I fall back because I don't want to make someone else do the heavy lifting. Because I've been left before."

She didn't flinch. "So have I."

We stood there soaked and uncertain.

The air between us was tighter now, but not angry anymore.

Just full.

She stepped back under the awning. Close. Not touching. But close.

"I like you, Elliot," she said quietly.

"But I will not pull teeth to get to know you. Do you want this relationship? Then show up. Flaws, baggage, clumsy attempts, and all."

I nodded. "Same goes for you."

She smiled faintly and sadly.

"You don't need to be perfect."

"Good," I said. "Because I'm currently wearing wet socks and emotional immaturity."

A breath of laughter escaped her. "God help us."

We stood there until the rain lightened to a drizzle.

When we finally started walking again, we didn't hold hands.

But we walked in step.

That felt like something.

Maybe not a resolution.

But a start.

THREE DAYS OF SILENCE

∞

Elliot

I thought I'd wake up the next morning to a text.

Something simple. A "still mad but thinking of you" sort of thing.

A joke.

A gif.

A breadcrumb.

Nothing came.

I told myself I'd wait.

That it was smart, mature, even, to give her space.

That this wasn't avoidance. It was respectful restraint.

But by the end of the first day, I was staring at my phone like it owed me an apology.

She was still in my mind.

Every quiet moment felt like it had her fingerprints on it.

Making coffee? I thought of the way she said, "Careful is safe."

Folding laundry?

I saw her green dress, how it swayed just slightly when she walked.

Even the pink sweatshirt, yes, I still had it, sat on the back of the chair like a silent dare.

I kept composing texts in my head.

Versions of an olive branch.

"Rain aside, that was a memorable walk."

"Are we really doing the silent treatment?"

"I miss you. There. I said it."

But I never hit send.

Pride is a hell of a thing.

It dresses itself up as self-respect and tells you that you're winning by standing still.

By Day Three, I wasn't even pretending anymore.

I missed her.

Not in the casual way.

In the-day-feels-strangely flat-and-muted way.

Like a colour had gone missing from everything.

But I still didn't text.

I wanted her to reach out first.

Because if she did, it would mean she cared enough to try.

Harper

On the first day, I expected a message. Not because Elliot was predictable, but because I thought I'd left enough space for him to meet me halfway.

I wanted him to.

God, I wanted him to.

Instead, all I got was silence.

I played it cool.

Went about my day.

Answered work emails.

Reorganised the kitchen junk drawer like a woman with a plan.

Ignored my phone whenever it lit up, then peeked at it like it might change its mind and deliver the message I was waiting for.

I hated that I was waiting.

I hated more that I missed him.

He'd made me laugh. He'd made me think.

He'd let me in, even if it were brief, messy, and reluctant.

I knew vulnerability scared him.

What I didn't expect was how much his silence would hurt.

By day two, I told myself I was fine.

I went to dinner with friends and smiled through it all, but every time someone asked, "So how's Elliot?" my stomach did a little backflip.

I lied with something breezy and non-committal.

"We're figuring it out," I said, like I wasn't counting how many hours had passed since the last time I saw his face.

Then, by day three, the quiet had gone from frustrating to heavy.

The thing is, I didn't want perfect.

I wanted effort.

A simple, human, flawed effort.

But I would not chase someone who folded the moment things got emotionally complicated.

Not again.

Not after the relationships where I'd done all the reaching.

So, I stayed quiet, too.

Even though I missed the sound of his voice like a favourite song, I couldn't replay it.

Elliot

The pink sweatshirt mocks me now. Every time I pass it, I hear her voice.

"So, you have an excuse to come back."

It had been a half-joke. A throwaway line.

But now I wanted an excuse.

Hell, I wanted to return the sweatshirt just so I could see her again.

When you think of it, three days isn't long. Not in the grand scheme of things. But when you're in the middle of it, when you're caught in the pull of "should I or shouldn't I?" it feels like a chasm.

I told myself if she texted, I'd be gracious and understanding. I'd say I missed her, too.

But she didn't text.

Neither did I.

Instead, I carried her around all day like a thought I couldn't finish.

And maybe—just maybe—I didn't want to finish it without her.

Harper

By the end of day Three, I stood at my kitchen sink washing a single mug and wondering what it would've been like to have him here, teasing me for putting oat milk in my tea or stealing the last cookie and pretending he thought it was the first.

I missed his face when he was about to say something sincere and immediately followed it with a joke to soften the landing.

I missed the way he looked at me—like he wasn't sure what he'd done to deserve this moment but didn't want to waste it.

But he hadn't called.

He hadn't reached out.

And I didn't want to be the one to keep knocking on a door he wasn't sure he wanted open.

So, I dried the mug. Turned off the lights.

And stood by the window for a long time, staring into the rain as if maybe, somewhere out there, he was doing the same.

ALIN

∞

Three days of silence had done their damage.

My phone might as well have been a brick. I kept checking it like a reflex I hadn't unlearned. My apartment was too quiet. The pink sweatshirt remained untouched, folded with intention and waiting on the back of a chair like it might whisper encouragement if I stood near it long enough.

Something had to give. And I knew it had to be me.

But texting felt insufficient.

Cheap, even.

After everything.

After her eyes in the rain, the way her voice had dropped when she asked for something real.

She wanted effort. Something flawed. Something human.

So, I got in my car.

Not to drive to her place — I wasn't that dramatic — but to take a small gamble.

I went to her bookshop knowing the time she went to lunch. I had planned exactly what to do down to the last second.

I parked a block away, stepped inside, and immediately felt watched by a calico cat on the counter.

"Looking for anything in particular?" the woman behind the counter asked.

"Yeah," I said. "Do you have a copy of A Night of Love by J. F. Nodar?"

She nodded toward the back wall. "Third shelf from the top, under 'N.' Used to be one of our most stolen titles, believe it or not."

I smiled.

I found the copy quickly.

A hardcover. Fancy dust jacket.

I flipped to page 273, the one Harper had once called "The moment everything starts unravelling, and you can't stop reading." She'd told me that over coffee the week before our first date.

Then, from my coat pocket, I pulled out the note I'd written.

Folded neatly.

Nothing fancy.

Just ink on paper.

A voice in my hand, not a screen.

Harper,

I'm sorry for the silence. I've missed you—more than I know how to say over the phone. So, I'm trying something different. This isn't a grand gesture. It's just me. Showing up. Flawed, unsure, still learning. But here.

If you ever want to talk—bookstores, rooftops, rain or not— I'm around. And I'd really like to see you again.

Elliot

I closed the book and returned it to the shelf.

As I was leaving, the woman asked if I did not want the book, and I answered the manager should check the book for these is a note stuck in it.

She shrugged her shoulders as if she did not care, and I left the shop with my heart hammering against my ribs like it wanted out.

Then I waited.

Not for a text. Not right away.

Just waited.

She messaged me two hours later.

Harper: "This was creepy or lovely. I'm leaning lovely."

I almost dropped my phone.

Me: "I'll take lovely with a side of 'mildly weird.'"

Harper: "A secret handwritten note in my favourite book? That's bold."

Me: "Bold is new for me. Is it working?"

Harper: "Yeah. I think it is."

My fingers hovered over the keyboard, still unsure whether we were standing on unsteady ground or just rediscovering where it had been all along.

Me: "So... want to see a movie?"

There was a pause.

Then.

Harper: "Actually, yes. The Roxy's doing a special screening of Alien this weekend. 47th anniversary. Sigourney Weaver in space and tank tops. It's a whole thing."

I blinked. Twice.

Me: "Alien??"

Harper: "What, did you think I was only into sad indie dramas and vintage bookstores?"

Me: "Yes. And maybe documentaries about French cheese."

Harper: "Shame. I'm a woman of many contradictions."

I stared at the screen, grinning like a lunatic.

Me: "Then let's go. I'll bring popcorn. I am not paying those outlandish prices for it. You bring the unapologetic nerdiness."

Harper: "Deal. Meet you there."

The Roxy was already buzzing when I arrived.

Retro posters, a cardboard cut-out of Ripley with a flamethrower, and more people in xenomorph-themed T-shirts than I thought existed outside Reddit.

Harper showed up in jeans, a black leather jacket, and a ponytail.

She looked like the cool girl in a graphic novel. The one who knows things before the protagonist does and doesn't care if you catch up.

"I brought snacks," she said, holding up a small paper bag. "Contraband gummy worms. We're living on the edge."

"I brought homemade popcorn," I added.

"Look at us. Rule-breakers with snack-based priorities."

We found seats in the middle row. It was her pick.

"So, you get full screen but not neck strain," she explained. We settled in, the lights dimmed, and the movie began.

I watched the opening credits, sneaking glances at her face lit by the flickering screen.

She mouthed lines she already knew. Grinned during tension. Squeezed my arm reflexively when the first jump scare hit.

She was alive in it.

Entirely herself.

And I couldn't stop watching her, even when I should've been focused on the killer alien stalking the crew of the Nostromo.

Midway through, she leaned over.

"I was obsessed with Ripley as a kid," she whispered. "She wasn't just strong. She was smart. Terrified but never frozen. That stuck with me."

I nodded.

It made sense.

Harper didn't posture or pose.

She moved through the world with a quiet, deliberate strength. She wasn't afraid of being afraid, so long as she was moving forward.

When the credits rolled and the lights came up, we stayed seated for a moment.

"I didn't expect to learn that about you tonight," I said.

"What, that I'm a sci-fi geek?"

"That you're full of surprises. And a little terrifying."

She smiled, tucking her legs beneath her. "You learn something new every time."

"I'm starting to like that."

We exited into the night, the street slick with leftover rain. The neon from the Roxy sign cast everything in a purple-blue glow. She looked over at me, a smirk playing at the edge of her mouth.

"So," she said, "was this more fun than moody bookstores and awkward rain fights?"

"Honestly? I think I needed both." I spoke.

We walked in silence for a moment.

A wonderful silence this time.

Then I stopped.

"I meant what I wrote," I said.

"About wanting to see you. Not because I think I have it all figured out. But because I know I want to keep figuring it out with you."

She didn't answer immediately.

Just looked up at me with that unreadable expression she wore when she was parsing something carefully.

"I want that, too," she said at last. "But just don't disappear when it gets messy, okay?"

"I'll stay," I said. "Even when I'm awkward. Even when I'm unsure."

She smiled.

"Then," she said, "you can keep the pink sweatshirt a little longer."

I laughed. "That thing's going to be in my will if we keep this up."

We stood at the curb, watching the streetlights blink like Morse code.

No kiss goodnight this time.

Just her hand slipping into mine as we crossed the street—quiet, easy, deliberate.

And for now, that was more than enough.

THE INVITATION

Three weeks.

That's how long it's been.

Three weeks of talking late into the night, voices low and tired but unwilling to hang up.

Three weeks of texting first thing in the morning.

Sometimes playful, sometimes thoughtful, sometimes just a simple "thinking of you" in the middle of the day.

Three weeks of WhatsApp video calls where we did nothing special, just existed in each other's space from afar—she is cooking, me cleaning up the kitchen, both of us pretending we weren't completely captivated by each other's small, ordinary movements.

And in all of that, I could feel something changing in me.

I was coming out of hiding.

Not all at once.

Not dramatically.

But slowly.

Steadily.

Like thawing.

Like spring stepping into a place that had forgotten the sound of birdsong.

And Harper, well, she noticed.

She didn't say it outright. She didn't need to.

It was in the way her voice softened when she greeted me.

In the way, her eyes lingered longer on the screen.

In the small, unspoken confidence she carried when she sent me a selfie in her glasses and said, "This is what I look like when I'm not trying."

I liked it.

I liked her.

And she knew.

When she invited me to her place for dinner, Saturday night, just us, no theme, no event, just the two of us and whatever that night turned into, I didn't hesitate.

I said yes.

She opened the door in bare feet and a soft sweater that hung a little off her shoulder. Her hair was loose, and she was wearing no makeup, or maybe she was wearing the kind that looks like nothing but probably takes skill to pull off. The house smelled of basil and something roasting in the oven. The lights were low, the music something warm and jazzy.

It didn't feel like a seduction.

It felt like a welcome.

We talked over wine, leaning against the kitchen counter while she checked the oven and I offered to help but mostly just stood there admiring her ease.

Everything between us felt settled in a way I hadn't expected.

Like the nerves had taken a step back to make room for the truth of things.

After dinner, with the plates barely cleared and the glasses half-full, we settled on the lounge. She tucked one leg beneath her, turned toward me, and asked the question that had been hovering for weeks.

"What do you want out of this? Out of this relationship?"

I didn't stall.

I didn't deflect.

I looked her in the eye and said it.

"Passion. Intimacy. Commitment."

The words weren't rehearsed.

They came from somewhere beneath the usual armour.

The place that wanted her to know me. All of me.

The place I wanted all of her.

She held my gaze. And then she smiled slowly, almost shyly.

"That's what I want, too."

And then she leaned in.

The kiss was different this time.

There was no preamble, no second-guessing.

No tension waiting to be resolved.

Just this moment, fully present, her mouth on mine, her fingers sliding into my hair, and my hands tracing the curve of her waist as if my palms had been waiting for the shape of her.

It was gentle at first.

Curious.

Then deeper.

Fiercer.

All the tension that had built over three weeks, the restraint, the distance, the unsent messages, the almosts, and maybes melted into heat.

The kind that hums in your chest and pulses in your fingertips.

She broke the kiss only to look at me, her breath warm against my cheek.

Then she reached for my hand.

"Come with me," she whispered.

I followed her through the quiet of the apartment, past the books and soft lighting and half-finished puzzle on the table, to her bedroom.

The door didn't close behind us with a dramatic click. It stayed open, as if even the house knew something intimate and important was about to happen.

She stood in front of me, eyes searching mine, giving me that last opportunity to hesitate.

I didn't.

I touched her face gently, reverently.

Kissed her again, slower now.

My hands exploring with intention, not urgency. Hers moving across my shoulders, slipping beneath fabric, tracing the lines of someone she was no longer guessing at.

There was nothing rushed.

No need to impress, no pressure to perform.

Just the two of us, undressing each other with a kind of tenderness I didn't know I was capable of.

The warmth of her skin against mine sent a slow ache through my chest.

The curve of her hip beneath my hand felt like something sacred.

The look in her eyes, open, wanting, sure, was the most beautiful thing I'd ever seen.

When we made love, it was quiet.

Not muted. Not shy.

But unspoken in the best way.

Breaths, touches, the rhythm of two people teaching each other with wonder instead of fear.

We moved together as if there had been no one else before.

Or if there had been, they were only shadows leading us here.

She whispered my name once, soft, and sharp, like it surprised her how deeply she felt it.

I kissed her shoulder, her throat, the hollow beneath her collarbone. She arched into me, eyes closed, hands gripping the back of my neck like I was something to hold on to.

I continued savouring each inch of her body. Kissing her, nibbling her until I kissed where it mattered most, and she moaned. I eased myself into her gently, and we rocked together as one.

When it ended, we didn't move for a long time.

She curled into me; the sheets tangled around our legs, her fingers tracing slow circles on my chest.

"I wasn't expecting that," she said, barely above a whisper.

"Me neither."

And I meant it.

This didn't feel like a moment.

It felt like a beginning.

We lay there, heartbeats slowly synchronising, silence folding around us like a warm blanket, then she spoke.

"Elliot, you've changed, and I like what I see."

"Well, Harper, I feel that whatever it is we are building in this relationship has just found a deeper foundation. Tonight, I felt everything I am looking for in a relationship. Passion, intimacy, and commitment. And you?"

"Likewise."

"I guess we will continue to find out more about ourselves, Harper. Are you interested in that?" I asked.

"Yes. Let us dig deeper into our souls and know each other more."

When she said that, all I could think was neither of us wanted to stop digging.

THE FAMILY ROAST

Harper gave me a full 48 hours' warning before D-Day. Dinner Day.

"Dinner at my parents' place," she said casually while brushing her teeth one morning. "Nothing fancy. Just you, me, my mum and dad, my brother, and my niece. Oh, and maybe wear something you wouldn't mind sweating through."

"Pardon?"

"They're delightful. And relentless. Think Sunday roast where you're the roast."

I laughed. Nervously.

And so, I spent the next two days overthinking everything.

My shirt, my handshake, whether I should bring wine, flowers, or just a laminated CV of my moral character. I settled on a bottle of Pinot and a pie from the bakery Harper swore by. I considered slipping in a note that said, "Please don't interrogate me," but thought better of it.

We arrived at a charming weatherboard house tucked behind an overgrown garden, the kind of place that held laughter in its walls and smelled like citrus polish and cooked onions.

As soon as Harper rang the bell, I heard the sound of multiple dogs barking (nonvisible) and a woman shout, "If it's that vacuum salesman again, I swear I'll take a broom to him!"

The door opened.

"Ah, it's the boyfriend," the woman said cheerfully, all menace gone.

"Hello, darling. I'm Margaret. You may call me Mrs Linton. Or Mum. Depending on how tonight goes."

Harper kissed her mother's cheek. "Mum, this is Elliot. Please try not to interrogate him until he's had at least two bites."

"I make no promises," Margaret said, ushering us inside.

Harper's father appeared from the lounge, tall, silver-haired, and suspiciously holding a notebook. "Ah, the interloper," he said, eyeing me over his bifocals. "I'm Ron Linton. Retired barrister. Still licensed to intimidate."

"Hello, sir," I said, extending a hand. He took it, measured my grip, and nodded with exaggerated solemnity.

"Firm handshake. That'll buy you eight minutes of mercy."

We entered the dining room, where Harper's brother, Will, was pouring wine while his teenage daughter scrolled on her phone with Olympian disinterest. The table was set with vintage China and an alarming number of cutlery options.

"This is Elliot," Harper said to the room.

Will gave me a chin lift. "So, you're the guy who sends her notes in books and all kinds of texts at all times of the night. At first, I thought you were fictional."

"Very real," I said. "Though arguably worse at texting than fiction would allow."

"Cool," said the teenager without looking up. "I'm Maddie. I've already stalked your Instagram. Not bad for a millennial."

"Technically, I'm a 'geriatric millennial,'" I offered.

Ron perked up. "Self-deprecating humour. Tread carefully, young man. That's how I courted Margaret. Now I've been laughed at for 52 years."

Margaret rolled her eyes. "And you've earned every one of them."

We sat.

Food arrived.

Roast lamb, mint sauce, and several side dishes that I tried not to confuse.

I was two bites in when the inquisition began.

"So, Elliot," Ron began, folding his hands like a judge about to issue a verdict. "What exactly do you do again?"

"I'm a writer," I said.

"Ah, one of those," he mused. "Writer is Latin for 'unemployed,' isn't it?"

Harper choked on her wine. I smiled.

"I actually work. I have published several novels, and they are paying the bills, and my subscription newsletter also helps financially," I said calmly. "I write romance, short stories, science fiction mostly."

Margaret jumped in. "And how long have you known our daughter?"

"Now about seven months," I said.

"About seven months," she repeated. "And yet here you are. At dinner. In our house. Breathing our air."

"Mum," Harper warned.

"I'm just saying!" Margaret said, gesturing with her fork. "We're old. We don't have time for slow burns."

"I like him," Maddie said. "He's got good eyebrows."

"Well, that seals it," Ron said. "A man with noble brows."

Harper caught my eye and mouthed, "You're doing great."

I pressed on.

"Look, I understand that this might feel fast. But I'll be honest with you. I didn't plan any of this."

Ron raised an eyebrow. "Any of what?"

"This," I said, gesturing to Harper beside me. "Her. Us. But she walked into my life as I was getting a coffee, and I've been spinning ever since—in the best way."

The table fell silent.

Then Ron leaned back in his chair, arms crossed. "So, what are your intentions?"

Margaret leaned forward. "Yes, Elliot. Enlighten us. What are your intentions with our daughter?"

Harper groaned. "Are you serious?"

But I didn't falter.

I looked directly at Ron, at Margaret, and finally at Harper.

"I believe I've fallen for your daughter, sir," I said.

"Utterly. Unexpectedly. And completely."

Harper blinked, surprised.

A flush rose on her cheeks.

Then, without missing a beat, she whispered:

"And I for him."

Margaret made a tiny squeal.

Maddie gave an approving nod.

Will muttered, "Well, now I feel single."

Ron, still silent, tapped the table with a single finger.

Then he smiled.

"That's more honesty than I was expecting from a man who wears loafers," he said.

"They're not technically loafers..." I started.

"Let the record show: we approve," Margaret said, beaming.

"Provisionally," Ron added. "Pending dessert."

Harper reached under the table and laced her fingers through mine.

I squeezed back, letting the moment settle around us like a warm blanket.

Later, as we were leaving, Margaret hugged me with surprising fierceness and whispered, "She deserves someone who sees her."

"I know," I whispered back.

Ron shook my hand again at the door.

This time, he clapped me on the shoulder. "Just don't screw it up, Elliot, because if you do, I will kill you."

"I'll do my best not to," I said.

As we walked to the car, Harper was quiet.

Thoughtful.

Then she said, "You said it. Aloud."

"I meant it."

She smiled and slipped her arm around me.

"So did I."

"You know, Harper, I felt like a teenager back there going through the Inquisition with your parents and family."

"I know. I was great, right?"

Yes, it was, I thought, and somewhere between her parents' interrogation and the roast potatoes, something had shifted again.

Something real had taken root.

And I couldn't wait to see what grew next.

UNPUBLISHED STORY

∞

Harper had the day off. I brought croissants and the good coffee beans she liked.

The ones she always said made her feel like she was in Paris and not three blocks from a dry cleaner that smelled suspiciously like boiled cabbage.

It was mid-afternoon, and the light filtered through her sheer curtains in a soft, golden way that made everything feel quieter, more thoughtful.

She wore one of those oversized shirts I suspected she had purchased in her twenties. It was soft, threadbare, effortlessly alluring in a way that made my heart stammer.

We were sitting cross-legged on the lounge, sipping coffee, a half-eaten almond croissant between us, talking about nothing and everything.

"Wow," I thought to myself, "How good silence could feel when you didn't have to fill it."

I stopped that thought and said: "Hey," I said, reaching into my bag, "I brought something."

Her eyes narrowed, playful. "Is it the pink sweatshirt? Because I've accepted that's yours now."

"No," I laughed. "Though I do wear it when I write. It brings me luck, obviously."

I pulled out a worn leather notebook.

Not my usual one.

This one had been with me for years.

It held things I didn't share. Rough ideas, late-night thoughts, half-formed lines that never made it into anything.

But somewhere in the middle, there was one piece.

One story.

"I wrote this about three years ago," I said. "Never showed it to anyone. Didn't even try to get it published. But I want you to read it."

She took the notebook, her expression softening instantly. "Now?"

I nodded. "I'll top up our coffees. Give you a minute."

I moved to the kitchen, pretending to fuss with the French press, but really just giving her space.

From where I stood, I could see her flipping pages, brow furrowed, mouth slightly open in that quiet, focused way of hers.

The story wasn't exceptionally long.

It wasn't even polished.

But it was honest.

It was about a man who thought he had everything figured out.

A man whose life unravelled in quiet ways.

Lost connections, lost direction, lost love that had grown cold and formal.

He drifted, not dramatically, but deeply. The kind of loneliness that doesn't announce itself. It just settles.

He failed.

In business.

In marriage.

In knowing himself.

And then, slowly, he started again.

No grand reinvention.

Just small choices.

New habits.

Kindness from strangers.

Long walks.

And eventually, someone new.

Someone who didn't fix him but who reminded him he could still be seen.

Of being wanted. Of being chosen, even with the cracks.

I wrote it when I was still too afraid to believe I could be any of those things again.

And now I wasn't afraid anymore.

I turned, coffee forgotten, just in time to see Harper close the notebook.

Her eyes were red-rimmed; her cheeks wet. She didn't speak immediately. Just stared at the leather cover like it had said something she wasn't ready to hear.

"I didn't expect that," she finally whispered.

"I know," I said, walking back to the lounge.

She handed me the notebook carefully, as if it were fragile. "That was beautiful. And brutal. And…"

"Too much?" I asked gently.

She shook her head. "No. Not even close. It just caught me off guard."

I sat beside her. Her hand found mine.

"You didn't mention anyone by name," she said. "The new person."

"I didn't need to," I said. "I think I was writing toward someone I hadn't met yet."

Her thumb traced a slow line across the back of my hand. "And now?"

"I don't need to write to anyone anymore."

She looked up at me then.

Really looked.

The way she did when she was trying to memorize the moment, not just experience it. Her expression was equal parts strength and tenderness.

"I love you," she said quietly.

It caught me off guard but not in the way that made me flinch. It settled over me like a home I hadn't realised I'd been walking toward all this time.

I leaned in, kissed her softly, then said it back.

"I love you, too."

What happened after wasn't rushed.

There was no frantic need, no desperate tug.

Just the closeness that comes when two people already know what the other needs without speaking.

She took my hand and led me to her bedroom. The light was still golden.

The room was warm and quiet; the air filled with the faint scent of her lavender linen spray and the lingering perfume of roasted coffee beans.

She kissed me slowly, deeply, like she was answering all the questions I hadn't yet asked. My hand found its way under her oversized shirt, and I was feeling the heat of her skin increasing, the tempo of her breath awakening and pulse increasing in my palm.

Clothes became an afterthought, peeled away piece by piece between kisses and quiet laughter, until we were bare and honest and entirely present.

The way we made love was like a continuation of the story I'd shared.

Unspoken but understood.

I traced every inch of her as if mapping a place that I already knew I'd return to. Her body responded with a softness that belied the strength I knew she carried. Her hands explored with certainty, anchoring me to her with every touch, every sigh.

There was nothing performative about it. No choreography.

Just connection.

When we moved together, it was slow, intentional, reverent.

Her legs curled around me, her hands in my hair, her mouth whispering my name like it was both a question and an answer.

We spoke little.

We didn't need to.

The pauses between our movements were full of meaning.

The way she held my face between her hands, the way I kissed the centre of her chest, the way we looked into each other's eyes without blinking or looking away.

And when we both came.

Shuddering, breathless, undone.

It felt like arriving somewhere we'd both been longing for without ever naming it.

Afterward, we lay tangled in each other, the afternoon light dimming into something deeper, more golden still. Her head was on my chest. My hand in her hair.

Neither of us said anything for a long while.

Then, softly, she whispered, "You should publish that story someday."

I smiled.

"I just did," I said.

CRACKS IN THE FOUNDATION

By the time we hit the six-month mark, things with Harper had grown into something deeper than I'd imagined. Not just in love but in a wonderful rhythm.

We had our routines now.

Late-night voice messages.

Morning check-ins.

Sundays were usually slow, coffee at her place or mine.

We shared music like postcards and TV shows like secret languages.

We'd even started leaving a toothbrush at each other's place. That quiet, domestic kind of intimacy that creeps up on you without fanfare.

But I'd learned by now that when things feel too easy, someone starts to feel the weight of it.

And that someone, this time, was Harper.

It started small.

A slight pause when I joked, "Imagine what we'll be like in a year."

A moment of hesitation when I suggested she keep a drawer at my place.

A missed call or two.

An extra space between texts.

I didn't want to overthink it.

But that's what I do.

So, one night, over dinner at her place, Thai takeaway, low lighting, I said it.

"Do you think we're moving too fast?"

She froze for half a second.

Just long enough.

"Maybe."

There was a silence that wasn't hostile but wasn't warm either.

"I'm not saying I regret anything," I added quickly. "Just that it's been a whirlwind. And maybe we should be sure we're pacing ourselves."

She nodded slowly.

But her eyes shifted.

She stood up, walked into the kitchen, and returned with her glass of wine. Then she sat down cross-legged, elbows on her knees, posture folded in on itself.

"You know," she said finally, "I've always been the one people leaned on. My friends. My brother. Even my ex. People look at me like I've got it together, and eventually, they start depending on that like it's infinite."

I said nothing. I let her speak.

"I'm afraid," she said, eyes flicking to mine, "that one day you'll expect me to carry too much. To hold your whole heart as if it is mine to protect. And when I stumble, even worse, drop it, you'll look at me differently. Maybe even leave."

It hit me like a wave.

"I don't want to lean on you, Harper," I said quietly. "I want to stand beside you."

She looked away.

"Sometimes that's just a prettier version of the same thing."

And that's when it broke out of me.

"I'm scared, too," I said.

"Not of you failing me but of me being forgotten. Of becoming background again. I've been there, Harper. I've been the man who quietly disappeared from someone's life while they smiled and told me we were fine."

Her face softened.

"I'm terrified," I said, "of feeling like I matter one day and vanish the next."

We sat in that tension for a long time.

Not angry. Not broken. Just raw.

It was the most honest we'd ever been.

And maybe the most afraid.

Two days later, Harper's mother fell.

I got the call just after lunch. Harper's voice was thin. Fragile in a way I hadn't heard before.

"She's in the hospital. Head trauma. They're saying it's a coma."

I was already grabbing my keys.

By the time I got to the emergency wing, Harper was sitting in a plastic chair, her brother beside her, pale and stunned. Her dad was talking to a nurse, his composure cracking around the edges.

When she saw me, she stood up slowly, like her body wasn't sure what it needed to do. I opened my arms, and she walked straight into them.

She didn't cry.

She said nothing.

She just held on.

And for once, I didn't try to fix anything.

I didn't say, "It'll be okay," or offer silver linings.

I just let her be held.

I just stayed.

The next few days were chaos.

Shifts at the hospital.

Medical updates that were vague and terrifying.

Her mother's stillness under those machines.

Harper became a machine herself.

Efficient, focused, sharp.

But I saw it in her eyes: the exhaustion, the dread, the slow unravelling of someone holding it all together by force of will.

We barely talked about us.

There wasn't space.

She pulled back, not cruelly but with necessity.

Her energy went into her family.

Her worry, her guilt, her pacing in hospital hallways, hands in pockets, eyes fixed on the floor.

And I didn't know where to stand.

One night, a week into the coma, she snapped at me, and I'd suggested she take a night off from the hospital.

She turned on me, brittle and fierce. "Don't ask me to step away, Elliot. Don't try to manage this."

"I'm not," I said gently. "I'm just worried about you."

"I don't have the luxury of falling apart."

"I'm not asking you to fall apart," I said. "I'm asking if I can help carry it."

She looked at me as if she wanted to believe me.

She wanted to crawl into that sentence and rest there.

But she didn't.

She just said, "Not now," and turned away.

That night, I sat on my lounge at home alone, staring at the pink sweatshirt still folded on the armrest.

We weren't breaking.

But we were bending in ways I didn't know how to straighten.

I wanted to fight for her.

But I didn't know if she'd let me.

I just knew that love isn't always a bright, cinematic thing.

Sometimes, it's a quiet patience.

A waiting.

A presence.

And I still loved her.

Even in the distance.

Even in the dark.

SPACE AND STARS

$$\infty$$

Elliot

The decision wasn't sudden. It arrived quietly, after too many half-conversations and long silences, like the soft click of a door you hadn't realised was slowly closing.

"We need a little space," Harper said.

And I agreed. Not because I wanted to be apart from her but because being near her had started to feel like standing too close to a flame—drawn in but burning just the same.

So, we didn't say goodbye. We just paused.

I packed a small bag and drove north, away from the city to a little cabin I'd found on a whim—no Wi-Fi, no reception, just birdsong, silence, and a battered writing desk facing a grove of eucalyptus trees.

A retreat, I told myself.

But really, it was a retreat from—not toward—anything.

I spent the first day doing nothing. Then, slowly, I wrote. Not about us. Not directly. But about time. About grief. About love that doesn't vanish but changes shape—like water poured from one vessel to another.

I wrote in the mornings and walked in the afternoons. I made awful coffee. I stared at the trees as if they might offer advice. I missed her. Not desperately—but in that quiet, persistent ache you can't name and don't want to scare off.

I didn't check my phone. I didn't call.

I let the silence speak.

And I wondered every day whether she was thinking of me, too.

Harper

Maddie wanted stars. That's how this trip started.

"Can we go somewhere without streetlights and people yelling at each other from car windows?" She'd asked, looking up from her phone. "I want to see the actual Milky Way, not just Google Images."

So, I booked a weekend at a remote observatory campground where they had telescopes, bunk beds, and a healthy disregard for cell towers.

It felt like a pleasant distraction.

And it was.

Until the sky got dark and Maddie got curious.

We were lying on a blanket, necks craned toward the scatter of stars above, when she said, "Are you and Elliot broken up?"

I swallowed.

"No," I said. "We're just... on pause."

"That's not a real thing, you know," she said, still looking up. "It's like when people say, 'We're taking a break' in movies, and then someone sleeps with someone else, and everyone cries."

I turned my head. "Thanks for the vote of optimism."

She grinned. "I'm just saying. You looked really happy with him. Even Granddad said you were 'almost tolerable.' That's basically love from him."

I laughed in spite of myself.

Then Maddie turned serious.

"Do you miss him?"

"Yes," I said quietly. "Every day."

"Then why aren't you, like... together-together?"

I hesitated. "Because I panicked. It felt like I had to be everything to someone. And I wasn't sure I could."

Maddie was quiet for a moment.

"Do you think Elliot wanted you to be everything?"

I opened my mouth and then I closed it.

"No," I said. "I think he just wanted me to show up."

"Well," she said, pointing to the sky, "he's not a constellation. He's a guy. And he sounds like he really, really liked you."

I stared at the stars, Maddie's words heavy in the silence.

"Did you ever think," she added, "maybe you were afraid of needing him, not the other way around?"

That one hit deeper than I expected.

And I didn't have an answer.

The next day, I stood outside the tent and stared into the morning fog curling along the horizon, Maddie inside eating muesli and watching TikTok with no service like it was performance art.

I pulled out my phone and turned it on.

No messages from Elliot.

Just a home screen.

But I didn't need a message.

I knew I missed him. I knew I was ready to stop being afraid of how much I needed him—and how much I wanted to be needed in return.

It wasn't about being everything.

It was about being present.

Elliot

On the fifth morning of my retreat, I sat outside with my notebook and wrote a list of things I missed about her.

Not the big stuff.

The small, impossible-to-replicate details:

The way she tapped her lip when she was thinking.

Her habit of singing to the dog that lived across the street, even though it barked at her.

Her coffee order that changed every month like the seasons.

The way her laughter crested in two beats: a soft one, then the real one.

The exact way she said "Hmm" when she was stalling for time.

By the time I was done, my heart felt like it was knocking against the edge of my chest.

It wasn't fear anymore.

It was clarity.

I packed up my things that afternoon and headed back to the city.

Not to fix something.

But to begin again.

THE EMAIL

There are moments in life when you know, beyond doubt, beyond fear, beyond ego, that someone is yours—not in the possessive way but in the rightness of it. Like a lock recognizing its key.

I knew it back when Harper, somewhere between the third voicemail, when we started speaking to each other and she left me quoting obscure romantic comedies, and the night we slow danced on a rooftop to a song neither of us liked but didn't want to stop.

But love is tricky when two people have baggage.

Even trickier when the baggage has wheels and keeps trying to roll back into the room.

Still. I knew. And after that weekend in the woods, after missing her in ways that made no poetic sense, I decided it was time to say it. Really say it.

Not in a text. Not on a phone call. Not in the doorway of a hospital, or half-whispered across a pillow.

I was going to write it down.

Old school.

Unfiltered.

Possibly too long.

So, I made coffee, sat down at my desk, and opened a blank email.

To: Harper

Subject: Probably Too Long, But Also Very Much Me

Dear Harper,

Let me get this out of the way: this isn't a "we need to talk" email.

This is an "I've done a lot of thinking, and I haven't exploded, which is a good sign," email.

I've spent the last few days away from you, trying to clear my head, write some words, and pretend I'm not just refreshing your profile picture in my mind like a lovesick teenager. Spoiler: I am.

You once told me you're afraid of being depended on. That if someone leans too much, they'll eventually fall, and it'll be your fault for not holding them up.

I get that.

I told you I'm afraid of being forgotten. Of being someone who once mattered and then... doesn't.

You nodded, like you'd seen that happen to someone you loved once, and it scared you, too.

We both have our armour. Yours is independence. Mine is self-deprecating charm and exiting stage left before the lights come up.

But here's the thing:

I don't want to be the guy who's always packing emotional parachutes "just in case."

And I don't want you to think love means becoming a full-time caretaker for someone else's insecurities.

I want us to meet in the middle.

Half armour, half open hands.

I want to lean but not fall.

And I want you to rest, without having to carry me.

I want the mess and the Sunday mornings and the awkward silences when one of us is in a mood and the other's just trying to find the remote.

I want the real stuff.

I want you.

Also, I want to add (because this is a full disclosure email); I have developed a genuine, unshakeable affection for your niece Maddie, despite the fact that she terrifies me a little and would 100% outwit me in a debate about feminism and memes.

I miss you.

I miss your "hmm" that means you're pretending to think when you've already decided.

I miss your laugh when you're not trying to be charming.

I miss your weird habit of naming pot plants after obscure women in history.

I miss being near you.

If space is what you still need, I'll respect that.

But if you're ready, I mean really ready, I'd like to build something with you.

Not something grand or perfect. Just something real.

Something ours.

Yours (possibly, hopefully, still),

Elliot

I hit Send before I could second-guess a single sentence.

Then I stared at my screen for ten minutes like it owed me applause.

The next twelve hours passed in strange bursts of time. I tried to do laundry but just stood in front of the machine staring at the spinning clothes like a confused philosopher. I wrote a paragraph for a client and deleted it four times. I considered calling her and immediately chickened out.

Nothing.

No reply.

But I knew her. I knew she wouldn't write back immediately. Not because she didn't feel something, but because Harper reads carefully. She takes her time. She always has.

She reads with her whole heart.

I went to bed wondering if I'd said too much. Or just enough.

Woke up the next morning, checked my inbox.

Still nothing.

Then, around noon—just as I was about to lose the last of my composure—I got a message.

Not a reply. Not an email.

Just a text.

From Harper:

"I just went to Mum's home. She is fine. Back from the hospital. Been busy getting her settled back in. I read the email three times. I cried twice. I've been thinking. I have an idea."

That was it.

No emoji.

No punctuation beyond what was needed.

Just her. Steady.

Present. Thoughtful.

And an idea.

God help me, I love this woman.

MAYBE THIS IS SOMETHING

The email arrived at 6:43 AM.

From: Harper

Subject: Stop by the bookshop today. Trust me.

Just go sometime today. You'll know it when you see it.

Harper.

No greeting. No context. No punctuation fuss.

Just enough to tilt my heartbeat out of rhythm for the rest of the morning.

I sat there staring at the screen, coffee cooling in my hands, wondering if this was her answer.

To my email.

To everything.

I hadn't replied since her text the day before. The one that said, "I have an idea." I hadn't wanted to crowd it. To impede her process. She thinks in arcs. In quiet. In meaning.

Still, she had never sent me a breadcrumb quite like this.

So, by noon, I parked my car near the bookshop and was on foot, walking through with the focus that makes you forget how loud traffic is. The bookshop wasn't far. Just a few blocks from where she lived. An old bookshop that always smelled faintly of cinnamon, coffee, and forgotten jackets.

As I approached, I slowed.

And then I saw it.

In the front display window, right where the seasonal fiction usually lived beside the discount classics, stood a single book.

One copy.

Centred, lit gently from above.

Its title, in soft handwritten lettering:

Maybe This Is Something?

The author's name had been blanked out with a crisp strip of white tape.

But the rest of the cover...

It looked like a memory.

A watercolour sketch of two people dancing under fairy lights. One with a crooked smile, one with her hair falling over her face, barefoot, joy half-hidden. There was a steaming mug in the corner, a splash of red wine, and what looked suspiciously like a crumpled pink sweatshirt resting on the back of a chair.

I stood frozen, breath caught somewhere between awe and disbelief.

It was us.

It was our story.

I stepped inside.

The bell over the door jingled. The clerk, a girl in oversized glasses with a "Support Your Local Authors (Especially If They're Hot)" pin on her cardigan, looked up from behind the counter.

"Hi. Is Harper in?"

"You're Elliot, right?"

I blinked. "Yes?"

She smiled as if she'd just handed a winning lottery ticket to the right person. "One sec."

She ducked below the counter and reappeared with a small cream-coloured envelope.

Just my name, in Harper's handwriting. Slanted, neat, confident.

She said nothing else. Just passed it to me like it was sacred.

I opened it right there, standing awkwardly in front of the counter, hands trembling just enough to make the paper rattle. Inside was a single card.

Simple. Thick stock. Embossed around the edges.

It read:

Elliot,

So, this is me doing the thing I've always been afraid to do:

Telling the truth without cushioning it.

Saying how I feel without the soft edges.

I wrote something. Not for publishing. Not yet anyway.

I wrote it for you. For us. For the way we stumbled into something neither of us was looking for but both of us kept returning to.

You said you were afraid of being forgotten.

This is me saying:

You haven't been. You won't be.

I needed time to understand what I was holding in my hands.

Now I know.

I want to build something, too.

Something real.

And maybe—just maybe—something extraordinary.

Come over. I'll be home.

And yes, I have pie.

Harper.

I read it.

Then again.

Then, without a word to the clerk (though I think I gave her a dazed thumbs-up), I bolted from the bookstore and took off down the street.

I didn't wait at the next light.

I didn't check my reflection in the glass of passing shops.

I didn't hesitate.

I just ran.

Because when someone tells you they see you and they're still standing there, arms open, offering you a slice of pie and a second chance.

You don't walk.

You run.

BLTS AND BARE TRUTHS

∞

She opened the door wearing one of my shirts.

Just that.

Nothing else that I could see except bare legs and a quiet, steady look in her eyes.

No theatrics.

No declarations.

Just a woman who'd made a decision.

And me suddenly breathless, suddenly sure, standing on the edge of the rest of my life.

"Hi," she said, as though this was any other day.

"Hi," I managed.

"Come in," she said, stepping aside.

I did.

The door closed behind me with the softest click.

And then there was nothing but the air between us.

Charged but not frantic.

A low hum of knowing.

No apologies.

No questions.

Just this: two people stripped of all the second-guessing, all the excuses about timing or readiness or who might need whom too much.

We didn't speak for a while.

We didn't need to.

Her hand found mine, fingers warm and sure, and I followed her back to the bedroom like I'd been following her in a hundred other ways since the moment we met.

And when we made love, it wasn't like the first time, or the second.

It was as if time stood still.

The time we'd both been building toward, even when we didn't know we were.

Slow. Unafraid.

Not needing to prove anything, just wanting to be in each other's skin, breath, and orbit.

Every touch felt as if it was tethering us tighter.

Every kiss was like a promise.

We stayed wrapped in each other for a long while after. Her head was on my chest. My hand in her hair. Her legs tangled with mine like she had no plans of moving, ever.

And I didn't want her to.

Eventually, she stirred, kissed my shoulder, and said, "You hungry?"

I smiled. "Starving."

"BLTs?" she asked.

I could've cried.

"Goodness, yes."

We sat cross-legged on the floor of her lounge area, paper plates on the coffee table, two cold beers between us, and the best damn bacon-lettuce-tomato sandwiches I'd had in a decade.

She took a bite, wiped a bit of mayo from her lip, and said, "So, do we talk about it?"

I nodded. "Yeah. We probably should."

"Okay," she said, setting her sandwich down. "What does this mean? To you. Us. Now."

I looked at her, really looked.

Hair a mess, shirt sliding slightly off one shoulder, skin still flushed from before, eyes open and clear.

"It means I show up," I said. "Over and over. That's what love is, right? Not just the swoony stuff. But the boring, faithful, everyday part. The part where I make you tea even when I'm mad. The part where I fold your socks wrong but try again, anyway."

She smiled. "You're terrible at folding."

"I know."

She took a breath. "It means I stop running when it feels heavy. That I let you see the tired version of me. The one who doesn't always want to be strong."

"Good," I said. "Because I don't need you to be strong all the time."

"I used to think love meant carrying someone else's weight," she admitted. "Now, I think maybe it just means walking next to them while they carry their own. And sometimes swapping backpacks when it gets too hard."

"That's the most Harper metaphor I've ever heard," I said.

"You love it."

"I do."

She leaned forward and kissed me.

A soft, warm, full of lettuce-breath honesty.

We clinked beer bottles.

And sat there in the late afternoon sun, full of bacon and truth, knowing that this time wasn't a maybe.

This was something.

THE RETURN

The invitation came wrapped in Harper's usual brand of offhand charm.

"My parents want to have us over for dinner," she said one morning while I was at the stove failing to flip a pancake properly.

I turned, spatula mid-air. "Again?"

She smirked.

"Yes. You, me, Maddie, Will. Apparently, Mum feels well again and wants you to be there."

"Requesting me? Why do I feel like I'm walking into a second interview?"

"She claims she misses you," Harper said, stealing a bite of pancake. "But she also told me she owes her taxes."

"Pardon?"

"She's got a whole plan. Just go with it."

And that's how I found myself standing on the familiar porch of the Lintons' household, holding my bottle of wine and a bouquet of whatever looked the least funeral-like at the florist.

The door swung open before we knocked.

Margaret Linton, recovered and radiant, wearing a flowing kaftan and with the same mischievous glint in her eye as before her fall, stood in the doorway with her arms crossed.

She stared at me for a long beat.

Then, narrowing her eyes, she said, "You again."

I opened my mouth to speak.

"You're the tax collector, aren't you?"

Harper stifled a laugh behind me.

I tilted my head, deciding to play along.

"That depends. Are you prepared to discuss your outstanding pie-based deductions?"

Her eyes lit up.

"Not without my lawyer."

"I brought wine. Will that work as a bribe?"

She snatched the bottle from my hands and stepped aside.

"You may enter. But only because I'm feeling merciful."

"Grateful, ma'am."

"Don't 'ma'am' me, I'm barely eighty-four."

Harper leaned in and whispered, "Welcome back to the gauntlet."

We stepped inside.

The house smelled of garlic and rosemary, and the faint sound of jazz floated from the record player. Ron appeared from the hallway; his glasses perched on his nose and a crossword puzzle tucked under one arm.

"Ah," he said. "Mr loafers is back."

"It's good to see you again, sir."

He nodded, extended a hand, and gave me a firm handshake. "Glad you didn't scare her off."

"Trust me," I said. "She does the scaring."

He grinned. "Smart man."

Will greeted me with a highball in one hand and a one-armed hug. "Glad you came," he said. "Mum's been rehearsing that tax collector line for a week."

Maddie was already halfway through a bowl of olives in the corner and gave me a nonchalant wave. "Hey, Loverboy."

"Hi, teenager with no filter."

"Still terrified of me?"

"Deeply."

She nodded in approval.

Dinner was served not long after.

A feast of roasted lamb, roasted potatoes, two kinds of salad, and a sourdough loaf Margaret had allegedly baked from a recipe she "no longer remembered but was spiritually guided through."

We ate. We laughed.

No one mentioned hospitals or comas or the silence between phone calls. Everything just felt, well, easy. Real.

Like we'd all agreed, without saying it aloud, to live in the present instead of the shadows of the last few months.

Somewhere between the second helping of potatoes and the opening of a second bottle of red, the conversation turned.

Will was the one who did it.

"So," he said casually, "what do we all think about marriage these days?"

Harper nearly choked on her wine.

"Oh no," Margaret muttered. "We're doing this?"

"I'm just saying," Will continued, "people either get married too fast or not at all. I'm curious where everyone falls. I knew the moment I met Sylvia. We tried to pretend we did not, but we fell for each other in a second, I think."

Ron, unbothered, said, "Marriage is about resilience. You either learn to share a bathroom or you're doomed."

Margaret chimed in, "It's about tolerating someone chewing beside you for fifty years without snapping. That's genuine love."

Maddie, swirling her soda, looked up. "Do you think people know when it's the right person?"

Harper turned to me, curious but cautious. I felt her hand graze mine under the table, her pinky finger brushing mine.

I cleared my throat and looked straight at Margaret.

"Well," I said, "personally, I think if you can survive dinner with someone's family twice and still want to see them naked, that's probably the one."

Laughter exploded around the table.

Margaret raised her glass. "I'll allow it."

"But seriously," I added, quieter now, "I think real love is showing up. Not once. Not on birthdays. But every day. In small ways. Whether you're in Paris or folding laundry in your shared silence. And when you find someone, you want to do that with? You don't let them go."

The room went quiet for a moment. Not heavy. Just full.

Then Ron said, "Well, hell. Get this man another drink."

Later, while Will and Ron argued over who got the last slice of tart and Margaret recited her "If I'd known I'd live this long, I'd have married someone rich" speech, I stepped into the kitchen to rinse some glasses.

Out of the corner of my eye, I saw Harper and Maddie in the hallway, just out of earshot. Maddie tugged on Harper's sleeve and leaned in.

I couldn't hear everything.

Just a whisper.

Then Maddie said, a little louder, "So, is he committed to you or not?"

I froze mid-rinse.

Harper looked down at her niece and smiled.

Then nodded.

Just once.

I pretended I hadn't seen it.

But my heart?

It saw everything.

After we said our goodbyes and shared a dozen hugs, and Margaret insisted she will pay her back taxes when hell freezes over and she gets a foot massage ("One or the other, not both"), Harper and I drove back to her place under a sky filled with stars and soft city light.

She took my hand in hers.

"Are you okay?" she asked.

"I think I love your family," I said.

"Even your mum. Especially your mum."

"She's a menace."

"She's perfect."

Harper squeezed my hand.

"Thank you for showing up," she said.

"I told you," I said, turning to her, brushing her hair behind her ear. "That's what I do now. I show up. For you."

She looked at me with that softness that always took my breath and handed it back in pieces.

"Good," she said. "Because I'm not going anywhere either."

As I drove, I asked Harper a question that I never wanted to ask, but tonight I felt I needed to.

"Harper, what happened to Will's wife?"

She looked out the window for a moment, and I could see it was a sensitive topic. She turns to me and says: "Can you pull over so I can explain?"

Without a thought, I check for a safe spot to pull over and turn off the car and turn to Harper.

"Will met Sylvia when they were in their early twenties and fell head over heels for each other and married right away. After thirteen years of trying to have a family, they had Maddie, and we were all ecstatic."

Harper stops as if to catch her thoughts before continuing.

"Then, when Maddie had just turned two, Sylvia was diagnosed with acute myeloid leukaemia, and she quickly succumbed to the disease since she had no white cell count to combat an infection she got. She passed away two weeks after going into the hospital. Will has been taking care of Maddie ever since, all by himself, with some help every so often from Mum, Dad, and me. We helped so he could have some time for himself."

I take all of this in and then I add.

"He said nothing to me. Never mentioned it when we first met. I made a stupid assumption that he was divorced. I feel so dumb."

"Don't Elliot. He does not speak of it, but he has devoted his life to Maddie, and once she finishes her education in three years and she goes off on her own, I believe he will start living his life again. Well, at least I hope so."

"Thanks for telling me this, Harper. This way, I do not say the wrong thing at the wrong time."

She just smiles.

"OK, let's take me home," she said.

And neither of us needed to say anything more.

Because finally, we were on our way home.

119

MUGS, STARS, AND TRAIN THOUGHTS

It had been a while since I'd been offered something with real teeth.

A byline, a deadline, the buzz of a newsroom, even if only part-time. The call came just after breakfast, and before I had time to overthink it, I was on the train, heading into the Central Business District with my satchel slung over one shoulder and caffeine doing its shaky best to impersonate confidence.

The train rocked gently, a familiar rhythm that sometimes helped me write and other times just lulled me into deep, meandering thought.

Today, it was the latter.

I looked out the window, watching the city grow taller as we moved, steel and glass stretching toward the sky, and my mind—predictably, involuntarily—drifted to Will.

To what he'd lost.

To what he never saw coming.

Will didn't talk about it much. I'd just found out when I asked Harper the other night. Just the thought of how Sylvia had passed—quietly, cruelly, unexpectedly. "Such a waste," I thought.

I remembered the look in his eyes. Not broken. Just altered when he spoke. It told me something had happened and like an idiot; I thought he had divorced Sylvia. Thank goodness he had asked Harper to explain.

And sitting there on the train, moving toward some version of my old life while clutching this new one in my heart, I asked myself—what would I do if that happened to Harper?

The thought landed like a stone in my chest.

Would I keep writing?

Would I get out of bed?

Would I turn into someone who wandered the world with one hand reaching for something that wasn't there anymore?

Or would I be strong?

Would I carry her memory like firewood, like purpose?

I didn't know.

And I hated that I didn't know.

But I also understood something in that moment—something I hadn't dared say aloud before, even to myself:

I didn't just love Harper. I depended on loving her. It grounded me. Gave shape to the days. Lit the edges of my otherwise greying world.

And I never wanted to live a single moment not remembering that.

The train pulled into Town Hall, and I stepped off into the rush. Umbrellas, briefcases, people talking into Bluetooth earbuds as if they were narrating an action film.

I had about twenty minutes until the interview at the Courier building. Enough time for a detour.

There's this bookshop tucked into the ground floor of a building just off the station, Millstone & Co.

Not big, not shiny.

The place that smells like old bindings and lemon oil. I wandered in with little of a plan.

Just habit.

Curiosity.

And that's when I saw them.

Two ceramic mugs sitting side by side on a table near the counter, nestled between small poetry collections and tiny felted mushrooms that served no clear purpose.

One mug read:

"Virgo: Overthinks. Over plans. Over delivers."

The other:

"Sagittarius: Impulsive but charming. Definitely has a passport and snacks."

I stared at them, and honest to god, I laughed aloud.

They were us.

Completely. Ridiculously. Unapologetically us.

I picked them up, one in each hand, and stood there like a guy who'd just been smacked across the heart by the universe.

Not fate exactly.

But maybe a gentle nudge.

A cosmic wink.

A reminder that even in the everyday train rides and freelance interviews and retail mugs, there are symbols that say: You're on the right track.

I bought them. Didn't even ask for a bag. Just walked out holding both mugs like twin declarations.

And as soon as I hit the street, I placed them in my satchel, and I pulled out my phone.

She answered on the third ring, background noise buzzing behind her like a crowded café orchestra.

"Hi," she said, already laughing. "I'm knee deep in a shipment of cookbooks, and someone just spilled an iced chai on my left foot. What's going on?"

"I saw mugs," I said, breathless. "Us mugs."

"Wait—what?"

"Mugs," I repeated. "One Virgo. One Sagittarius. They were side by side. They were us. I don't know why, but I bought them."

"You're calling me about mugs?"

"Yes. And also, because I love you. And I'll keep saying that. I'll keep showing up. Mugs and all."

She was quiet for a moment.

Then: "You're lucky I'm wearing non-slip shoes. You just made me slide a little."

I smiled. "I mean it. You don't have to say it back right now. I just needed to tell you. Again."

"I love you, too," she said simply. "Even when you buy mugs like a man in a movie."

"They were beside each other, Harper."

"Obviously meant to be."

"Like us."

She paused. "Okay, now I'm sliding again."

I laughed. "How's the shop?"

"Controlled chaos. Two customers got into a passive-aggressive spat over the last sourdough starter guide, and Daphnee may have just sold a fantasy novel by describing it as 'emotionally volatile with dragons.'"

"So, thriving?"

"Exactly."

She was still smiling.

I could hear it.

That soft edge to her voice she only got when she was happy and pretending not to be giddy.

"You heading to your interview?" she asked.

"In five minutes. I just needed to call you. To tell you that this life we're building, even the small bits of it, I love it."

"I see them, too," she said. "And I'll see you tonight?"

"My place or yours?"

"Mine," she said. "You can bring the mugs."

"Deal. I'll tell you everything about the interview. Even if I crash and burn."

"If you crash and burn, I'll make you pancakes."

"I knew I kept you around for a reason."

"See you tonight, Elliot."

I hung up and stared at the phone for a moment.

Then at the mugs.

Then up at the city towering above me.

And I swear, for the first time in a very long time, I didn't feel small beneath it.

I felt exactly where I was supposed to be.

THE SIRENS ON VIEW STREET

There are moments when everything seems to align.

Your thoughts, your future, the rhythm of your life and, for the first time in a long time, I was riding one of those waves.

The interview at the Courier went better than expected.

Not just well, hell, almost perfect. They didn't just want a filler freelancer to cover dry municipal budgets or school council votes.

They wanted long-form stories.

Depth.

Local people, real lives, and the in-between of everyday humanity.

They wanted my voice.

It felt like something I could do alongside the novel without either bleeding dry. Something that wouldn't just pay bills but fill a unique part of me.

The part that wanted community.

Grounding.

Narrative beyond fiction.

As the train left the city, I watched the sun lean west across rooftops and felt the rare, delicious buzz of contentment. I'd barely stepped off the platform at my station before I pulled out my phone to text Harper.

"On my way to yours. News to share. Might require wine and unnecessary celebration."

No response yet.

Probably mid-latte-pour or buried beneath a new shipment of niche gardening memoirs or on her way home and did not hear the notification.

I didn't mind. I knew I'd see her soon. I just wanted to see her face when I told her. The quiet pride was in her smile.

The way she'd lean in like I'd just told her I had a secret worth treasuring.

I got to my car, tossed my satchel into the passenger seat, and hit the road with the windows cracked and my playlist on shuffle.

But when I reached the turnoff for View Street, the traffic slowed.

And then stopped.

At first, I thought it was construction as always.

Common, annoying. But then I saw the flashing lights.

Red. Blue. Ambulance. Police.

The entrance to View Street was cordoned off with a set of orange cones and a parked patrol car.

People stood on sidewalks, whispering. Watching.

My stomach turned.

Something cold and creeping slid beneath my skin.

Still, I tried to tell myself it wasn't what I feared. Couldn't be.

But as I passed the blocked intersection, I saw it.

The back of a stretcher.

Paramedics.

A familiar head of auburn hair.

Harper.

No.

I slammed the car into park without thinking and flung the door open.

I was running before my brain caught up. Toward the lights. Toward her.

"Harper!" I shouted.

A uniformed officer stepped into my path. "Sir! You need to stay back!"

"That's my partner—please, please—let me through!"

"Name?" the officer demanded, firm but not unkind.

"Elliot Travers. I'm her partner—her name's Harper Linton."

The officer turned briefly to check with someone by the ambulance, then looked back at me. "We can't let you on the scene. She's being taken to Campbelltown Hospital. That's all we can tell you right now."

"But what happened? Is she—?"

"She's conscious but in distress," he said gently. "That's all I can say."

I felt my heart explode into a thousand shards as I watched the ambulance doors shut. Sirens lit up the street.

And then she was gone.

Just like that.

I stood there, useless. Breath coming too fast. Hands shaking.

Then, I did the only thing I could think to do.

I called Ron.

He answered on the third ring, and I couldn't keep my voice steady.

"Ron—it's Elliot. It's Harper. There's been an accident. I—I don't know what happened. But she's being taken to Campbelltown Hospital."

Silence. Then Ron, calm but clipped: "We'll meet you there. Margaret and I will leave right now."

I hung up.

And drove.

Faster than I should've. Praying harder than I had in years.

At the hospital, time did what it always does in a crisis—it slowed to a crawl and then sprinted in bursts.

I arrived first. Was told she'd just been brought into Emergency.

"No visitors yet," the nurse said. "They're assessing her now. You'll be informed as soon as we can share anything."

I nodded, numb.

Then I waited.

And waited.

Ron and Margaret arrived fifteen minutes later. Ron's eyes were red, jaw tight. Margaret looked like she hadn't taken a full breath since she got the call.

"Did they say anything?" she asked.

"Just that she was conscious," I said. "That's all."

We sat.

We paced.

We stood in and out of each other's personal gravity, orbiting the same fear but not wanting to say it aloud.

The coffee from the machine was lukewarm and tasted like anxiety.

I kept picturing her face. The way she had laughed just that morning when she spilled cinnamon on her notebook. The softness of her hand on my chest the night before. Her voice on the phone just hours ago.

"See you tonight, Elliot."

What if tonight never came?

I shut my eyes. Told myself to stop. Told myself she was strong.

But I couldn't stop the images. I couldn't stop the ache in my chest.

I loved her.

God, I loved her.

And I hadn't even told her about the job yet.

After what felt like forever, a nurse approached.

"Harper Linton?"

We stood in unison.

"Please follow me," the nurse said.

So, we followed her in silence and were led to a big conference room and told to wait that someone would be in shortly.

For what seemed like an eternity, but it must have been just five minutes, another nurse walked into the room followed by two other individuals.

"Are you Mr Linton?" he asked me.

"No, I am Elliot Travers, her partner. These are her parents, Ron, and Margaret Linton."

"I am so sorry, but Ms Linton passed away on the operating theatre because of results of the brain's inability to function after her injury, a hit and run, I was told. This led to brain death or brainstem death, where the brain and brainstem cease to function. This can happen when the brain is so severely damaged that it can no longer sustain essential functions like breathing and heartbeat, even with life support. We did everything we could, but it was sudden, and we do not believe she suffered."

"But she was conscious. I saw her as she was being placed into the ambulance." I screamed.

"Yes, Mr Travers, but circumstances changed when she arrived. We are so sorry."

I nearly collapsed.

Margaret wept. Ron closed his eyes and whispered something I'll never know.

"She asked for Elliot before passing in the ambulance. I was told," the nurse added.

"I want to see her," I said.

She led me down the hall, past rooms filled with soft beeps and drawn curtains. When I entered, Harper was lying on the bed. Eyes closed.

I went to her and saw the IV in her hand, bruises blooming on her temple and collarbone.

I lay next to her and held her in my arms.

A few minutes later, Ron and Margaret came in and joined me.

I continued to hold her and kissed her knuckles like she might vanish if I let go.

Ron and Margaret were silent. Nothing was spoken. They have lost their child.

I held her hand, and for once, I didn't have to overthink a single thing.

I felt my life had ended right there and then.

FROM THE MOUTHS OF BABES

There are no words that can prepare you for standing at the front of a chapel, facing the faces of people who loved the same person you did.

No right way to hold your body, or your heart, in that moment.

Only breath.

Only memory.

Only grief.

It had rained that morning, just a light drizzle, barely enough to wet the footpath, but somehow it seemed right.

Like the sky had decided to mourn with us, but gently.

Not with thunder. Just with an ache.

The chapel was full. Friends. Neighbours. Customers from the bookshop who'd come not with obligation but with affection. People she'd touched, helped, listened to.

Ron and Margaret sat in the front row, holding hands, stoic in a way that only parents who've endured can be. Will sat beside them, shoulders stiff. Maddie beside him, her chin tilted up, determined not to cry in public.

And me?

I stood at the podium, clutching the paper I hadn't looked at since writing it the night before. My hands shook. My mouth was dry.

I looked out at them all, at the sea of eyes waiting to hear what I would say about the woman we had lost.

And then I started.

"I thought I'd be telling this story differently. I thought one day I'd be standing in front of a crowd, giving a speech at a book launch or a wedding toast or maybe some retirement dinner where Harper would roll her eyes at the fuss. I didn't think it would be here. And yet... here we are. Harper and I had plans. We were going to turn the guest room into a writing nook. She was going to teach me how to make sourdough properly—without cheating and buying starter from the farmers' market. We were going to visit Japan in the spring and eat too much ramen. We were going to adopt a dog. Maybe a cat, too, even though she said cats were 'secretly judging her choices in men.'"

Laughter. Quiet, but grateful.

I continued.

"She used to joke that we were star-crossed in a coffee shop kind of way. Virgo and Sagittarius. Order and impulse. Mugs and messes. But somehow... we worked. She taught me that love isn't about grand gestures. It's not about perfection. It's about showing up. Folding laundry together. Listening to someone's dreadful day even when yours was worse. Laughing at the same dumb joke for the fifteenth time because you know it matters to them. She taught me that love isn't something we fall into. It's something we build. Brick by brick. Morning by morning. And though our time was short, she gave me more than I could ever put into words. But I'll spend the rest of my life trying."

I don't remember sitting down afterward.

I just remember Margaret squeezing my arm as I passed her, eyes shining with something soft. Something maternal. Ron giving me a quiet nod. Will patting my shoulder with a firm grip that said: "You're one of us now."

The wake was held at Harper's bookshop.

Because, of course, it was.

Tables had been brought in, tea lights lit. Friends wandered through with plates and stories. People cried over shelves and laughed in corners, their voices echoing off the walls like echoes of Harper herself.

I stood near the front window for most of it, unsure what to do with my hands, or my heart. The mug display still sat where I'd last seen it. Ours—Virgo and Sagittarius—side by side.

I felt adrift. Like the earth had shifted beneath me and I was walking on something not quite solid.

And then Maddie appeared.

"Hey," she said, sliding beside me. She held a ginger ale in one hand, her phone in the other.

"Hey," I replied.

"You did good. With the speech."

"Thanks."

She looked up at me with her trademark teenage frankness. "You look like you're barely standing."

I tried to smile. Failed. "It feels like a dream."

"More like a nightmare."

We were quiet for a beat.

Then, out of nowhere, she said, "You know she'd be furious if you gave up now, right?"

I turned to her, startled.

"I mean it," she said, dead serious. "Harper always said you were the guy who turned pain into pages. That you didn't just write stories—you understood them. The messy ones. The ones people don't want to look at."

She shrugged. "So, if you stop now? If you stop writing, or living, or loving people just because this hurts—then it's like forgetting her. And she'd hate that."

I blinked.

How does a sixteen-year-old say something that knocks the air out of your lungs?

"How did you get so wise?" I asked.

"Books," she said. "And listening to my aunt."

I chuckled, throat tight.

"She loved you," Maddie said. "Like, annoyingly so."

"I loved her, too."

"I know."

She reached into her bag and pulled something out—a tiny, leather-bound notebook.

"She kept notes," Maddie said. "About the story you two were writing. I found it this morning in her desk. Thought maybe you'd want it."

I took it reverently and opened it to the first page.

Her handwriting.

My name.

The title: Maybe This Is Something.

I pressed the book to my chest.

And for the first time that day, I didn't feel lost.

Just sad.

Just human.

Just still, somehow, living.

That night, when the last candle flickered out and the bookstore doors were locked behind us, I returned to my place, sat at my desk, and opened a new document.

Not to escape the pain.

But to honour it.

To honour her.

Maddie was right.

Harper would never want me to stop.

So, I wrote.

One sentence. Then another.

And it wasn't the start of something new.

It was a continuation of something eternal.

MAYBE THIS IS EVERYTHING

It's raining softly today.

Not a thunderstorm, not some grand gesture from the sky. Just a hush of water tapping the windowpanes—steady, like breath. I used to dread rainy days. Now, I find comfort in them. Maybe it's the permission they offer to stay still, to linger in thought, to let memory walk freely through the house.

A full year has passed since we lost Harper.

And I use the word we purposefully because it wasn't just me.

Her family. Her friends. Maddie. This town.

We all lost something the day Harper Linton left the world.

But not everything was taken.

Some things remained.

Some things grew.

Grief, for one.

But also love.

And somehow, from the tangled vines of both, came something else: a new sense of meaning.

The novel is done.

Maybe This Is Something?

It sits printed and bound on the table next to me. The proof copy arrived last week, and I couldn't touch it at first. It felt like holding a ghost in paper form.

When I finally opened it, I expected to cry.

But I didn't.

Instead, I smiled.

And then laughed.

Because Harper would have flipped through it, muttering something like, "Good title. Took you long enough."

And then probably dog-eared a page just to irritate me.

It's not just our story, but, of course, it is.

The heart of it, the bones, the soul—it's all Harper. The way she challenged me. The way she asked questions no one else did. The way she showed up when life got messy, confusing, real.

I still talk to her.

Not in a weird way. Just aloud sometimes when I go for a morning walk.

Like last week, I finally figured out how to fix that scene in chapter seven. I said, "You were right. The line needed cutting."

Then I laughed because, of course, she was right.

She always was.

Today, I talked to her again.

Standing at the kitchen counter, waiting for the kettle to boil. I looked at the calendar.

One year.

One breath.

One quiet ache behind the ribs.

And I whispered, "We made it."

I've started to live again.

Not just in the mechanical, wake-up-and-go sense.

But really live.

I reopened my old writing workshop with some friends. Started teaching again. Seeing stories take root in others the way Harper helped them bloom in me—it's healing in ways I didn't expect.

Maddie comes over often.

She reads everything I write.

Offers sharp critiques and warmer encouragement.

She's taller now. Her hair's shorter.

But her spirit?

Still pure Harper.

She asked me once, just a few weeks ago, "Do you still love her?"

And I said, "Always."

Then she asked, "Will you love someone else someday?"

I paused.

Thought carefully.

"Maybe."

"Good," she said. "Because she'd be pissed if you didn't even try."

Smart kid.

Ron and Margaret came over for dinner last Sunday.

Ron brought his lasagna, which Margaret still insists is "just okay," and I brought out a bottle of red Harper once hid behind the coffee beans in my pantry.

Will came and had a new friend, Wendy. They looked like a good couple. I am happy for him.

We sat in the backyard until late, telling stories, even the embarrassing ones. Especially those. Margaret told one about Harper's first driving lesson, which ended with a mailbox in someone's front yard never being the same again.

We laughed.

A genuine laugh.

And I realised something.

Healing doesn't mean forgetting.

It means remembering without breaking.

This morning, I stood at the big window in my office.

The house is still hers in a thousand small ways. Her photos, the plant she over watered that refuses to die, the record player she insisted I fix because "analog is charming."

I held my coffee in the Virgo mug.

The Sagittarius one—hers—sat across from me on the desk, filled with pencils. I've never used it for anything else.

The final sentence of the novel echoed in my head.

I'd typed it months ago, but it still lands like a prayer every time I think of it:

"Maybe love isn't about happy endings. Maybe it's about being brave enough to begin again."

I exhaled.

Watched the trees dance in the light rain.

The street was quiet. Still. Whole.

And then I said it.

Not in a whisper.

Not through tears.

Just simply.

Clearly.

To the surrounding space that still feels like her.

"Harper, maybe this is everything."

ABOUT THE AUTHOR

José F. Nodar

Flung into one of life's biggest challenges at just eleven, José's story began in Havana, Cuba. The Cuban revolution forced him onto a plane alone, landing him at an orphanage in a small Georgia town called Washington. Reuniting with his parents wouldn't happen until he was eighteen, a high school graduate in Atlanta.

Business Administration became his focus at Georgia State University. From there, he navigated the world of finance, first at the First National Bank of Atlanta (now Wells Fargo) and later as a project manager in financial consulting. These roles took him across the United States, Europe, and even Australia.

It was in Camden, New South Wales, Australia, that a spark ignited José's creative side. A writers' group became the launching pad for his debut novel, and soon, his mind birthed Danny Monk, his first major character.

But José's life isn't all about writing. When he's not crafting captivating stories, you might find him at the local mall, observing the world and gathering inspiration for future characters. Away from his computer, he dives into books or enjoys long strolls around Spring Farm.

Copyright © 2026 by José F. Nodar

Other books by José F. Nodar

English

- Books, Pens & Larceny
- Mending Hearts at Crystal Cove
- A Love Finally Spoken
- The Legacy Compass
- The Universe Between Us
- The Time Bus
- SEX
- The Compass Legacy
- The Teacher's Assistant
- Stories to Share with My Partner Book 1
- Stories to Share with My Partner Book 2
- Stories to Share with My Partner Book 3
- Stories to Share with My Partner Book 4
- Stories to Share with My Partner Book 5
- Stories to Share with My Partner Book 6
- Stories to Share with My Partner Book 7
- Stories to Share with My Partner Book 8
- Stories to Share with My Partner Book 9
- Stories to Share with My Partner Book 10
- Stories to Share with My Partner Book 11

Spanish

- Cuentos Para Compartir con Mi Pareja Libro 1
- Cuentos Para Compartir con Mi Pareja Libro 2
- Cuentos Para Compartir con Mi Pareja Libro 3
- Libros, Bolígrafos y Hurto
- Reparando Corazones en Crystal Cove
- Un Amor Expresado
- El Autobús del Tiempo